The People Inside Me: Autobiography of a Red-Brick House

Susan M. Szurek

Chapbook Press

Schuler Books
2660 28th Street SE
Grand Rapids, MI 49512
(616) 942-7330
www.schulerbooks.com

The People Inside Me: Autobiography of a Red-Brick House

ISBN 13: 9781966196563

eBook ISBN 13: 9781966196570

Library of Congress Control Number: 2026903481

Printed in the United States.

Also by Susan M. Szurek*

Everstille: A Novel

Everstille's Librarian

Olivia from Everstille

Tomas' Children

Her Cousin Julia

My Brother's Things

A Thousand Fibers

*Books available at Chapbook Press
(https://www.schulerbooks.com/chapbook-press)
at Amazon, and other online book sellers.

To Raymond Pietras

who may not have lived in a red-brick house

but was a neighbor and friend

for thirty-five years.

S.M.S

There is no place like home.

L. Frank Baum

L. Frank Baum is an idiot.

The Red-Brick House

The Parts of My Book You Will Read:

1

My Beginning, 1886

I am.

Despite my age, one-hundred-and-thirteen years, I am as strong as the year I was built. Actually, I am stronger due to the repairs such as new roof, tuckpointing, updated windows. And now, with additional renovations and updates being completed by the new humans (Not *owners*. I am owned by no one.), I am sure I will stand for at least another century. But I am getting ahead of the story. Allow me to begin at the beginning. You will be interested.

The beginning. First, let me qualify myself. I am not just a *Workers Cottage*, although some have called me that. I prefer to be called *Victorian*, although I am, admittedly, simpler than that structure. I do not claim to be *Italianate* and am certainly not *Tutor*. Both housing styles, to my understanding, are considered pretentious due to their European appellations. They are North Side styles, pompous and snobbish. That is the scuttlebutt whispered by the other houses, streets, and alleys, and I agree. Perhaps *Workers Cottage* is the correct designation. It is, after all, a substantial and honest one. And I am a substantial and honest South Side construction, not of wood, but of solidly crafted brick. I am a red-brick house. Yes, I have the Chicago common brick on my sides and back, but my face brick is a wonderful hue, deeply and smoothly red, created with high amounts of iron oxide, and still, after more than a century, majestically vivid. I was built facing Western Boulevard. The Boulevard, with whom I rarely communicate, was called that because a couple decades before I was built, that street area marked the western border to the city of Chicago. The Boulevard informed me of that fact. Of course, the city has expanded greatly over the last century, and I have been here to watch it, to view the changes, to remain upright and strong. I am not bragging. That is a human characteristic, not mine.

At my start, my plot was measured and marked. The foundation was laid, and at that point, I achieved awareness. I am not human; I do not possess the spindly feelings humans have; I do not become glad or angry or expound the braggadocio, a human convention I have observed. I am simply aware. As my framing was completed, the rough plumbing and other work done, my inside and outside slowly came together, I remained perceptive and observant. There is no accounting for this. This is not magic or supernatural. I am a sentient, well-built, red-brick residence, able to observe and not judge, to understand and not misinterpret, to hear and not misconceive, and that is all. I simply am. To analyze or wonder about this is a waste of time and consciousness. I say that without arrogance or condescension. Do not ponder it unnecessarily.

My insides. I am spacious. Once the large outside front doors open, there is an entryway, a slight room, which allows for wet hats and coats, muddied boots and shoes, drippy umbrellas; all can be stored and dried. It is lengthy and simple, containing a small table and coat rack for necessary items. Windows on either side enable outside light to enter my front parlor which has a bay window facing west. Immediately to the north, there is a staircase which travels to the upstairs rooms. More on those rooms later. Just inside the parlor on the north wall, is a door leading to the first bedroom. A fireplace stands across from the bay window, and built-in bookshelves are on either side with ample space for additional furniture. There is room for a settee, some chairs, and a large table centered in the bay area. Of course, the furniture came later, and over the decades was often changed, but the plaster on the walls, the ornate molding, the high woodwork, the carefully wrought baseboards against my flooring remains. There is a separate story about the plasterwork.

My ability to understand human speech, no matter which language was spoken, came naturally with my awareness. I could understand the various foreign languages and dialects immediately. Again, do not wonder, just accept. I did. There were many workmen whose hands created me, but I admit to some favorites. There were two Irish fellows, a father and son, who created my plaster work, and as they shaped it, the older man taught the younger one, cautioning him, correcting him, making him do things over until he was satisfied with the outcome. They were not supposed to add the coving or the ornamental plasterwork, but the old man took it upon himself to use the space as a teaching tool. I didn't mind; it was becoming to my room. And they only did it to the front parlor. I would listen to the conversation which, even in their heavy Irish brogue, was understandable to me. The father was not always a kind teacher. He was harsh at times, grabbing tools from the son's hands, upset at the son's inexpert nascent work.

"Let me show yer' oy ter chucker dat," and he would complete the swirled rose with just a few strokes.

"But owl lad, oi already did dat," and the son would complain.

"That's not roi; quit actin' the maggot…*Amadán!"* would be the answer, and then the son had to complete the task again. Once the old man was satisfied, he would nod his head. Sometimes he would, in Gaelic, give the highest praise to the son. *"Sin thu fhéin"*. It didn't happen often, but when it did, I saw a sideways smile on the boy's face. And the attractive plasterwork remains.

An archway opens to the dining room, and on the northside wall was another door which led to the second bedroom. Across the southern wall was a built-in sideboard where rarely-used but precious china was stored. A large dining table and chairs were the centerpiece of the room. Another curved archway led to a small hallway and the indoor bathroom, and on the other side of that hallway was an additional small room meant for a housekeeper or young child. The elongated kitchen area was to the south of the small room. A work area, a stove, and a sink took up the east wall. A counter and a space for an ice box, and in later years, an electric refrigerator, was located on the west wall, and a pantry at the south end of the kitchen fitted snuggly between the walls. I contained whatever newness was available in 1886, and my rooms were updated through the decades. I must admit that the indoor bathroom was special, and some of those North side *Italianate* houses did not contain one until the century turned. So I heard.

Next to the small room meant for a housekeeper, was the back staircase which traveled to the second floor. Two staircases, as it turned out, was a prudent addition. Also, a mistake. But that story will be told. There was a back door leading out of the kitchen which opened into an indoor porch area. It was mostly used for storage, and the windows across the back wall gazed out into the yard where the tree which was allowed to remain, stood tall in the middle. There had been another, but because it was too close to my foundation, it had been removed. A free-standing garage was eventually built, but that did not happen for some years. Once it was built, the fencing along the back needed to be replaced, and the alleyway could no longer be seen. I had no problem with that. I never thought much of the alleyway's dirty cinders which were sometimes dragged from the bottom of shoes onto my flooring.

There was a staircase from the back storage porch to the outside, and another from the outside to the basement garden apartment. A door from the walkway on my south side opened into the apartment, and various small windows were placed low along the sides, allowing for light to enter. The space for the apartment was created, but no rooms were completed for decades because the original humans had run out of funds. When it was completed and rented, it often contained families with children. Children. They cried and were dirty and noisy and some of them marked up my walls or chipped them using their toys. Never cared for them.

Now to the upstairs rooms. Originally there were two large rooms next to each other connected by a door between them. They were first used as separate bedrooms, although later that changed. I will get to that. Across the hall from the rooms was another partially finished indoor bathroom and on either side were spacious storage closets. Down the hallway which curved around in a clever way, was the back staircase which led to the kitchen. Altogether I contained eight rooms, two indoor bathrooms, a number of built-ins, two staircases, a large garden space for the eventual apartment, and an entry way. Now really, should I be called a *Workers Cottage*? Admittedly, the people who built me and subsequent other humans who resided in me, were workers. It was necessary, I suppose, for them to work to support themselves, their families, and take care of me.

I was created shortly after the house on the lot to my north was built. It, too, was red-brick, but, and I claim this only because it is true, its brick was not, and is not, nearly as vibrant as mine. Houses claim no gender, but if I were to name one for the north-lot house, it would be male. Older, quieter, wearier, not particularly…umm…alert. We rarely communicated. A walkway separated us. It traveled down the gangway between us, ending at the alley. A small fence surrounded his yard which was never kept up as carefully as mine. It contained no tree, and although an attempt had been made to brighten the dull place up with a few plants, they were never cared for, and that neglect may be the reason for his reticence, his backwardness. A couple of decades after I came into being, a house was created on the empty lot to my south. It was a yellow-brick, rather cheap, if I am being truthful, and I always am, and I would gender it female. A loud and common female, thinking herself lovely and delicate, but I can see her sloppy mortar work on the sides where it was hurriedly done, and the second window on this side is not plumb. At first there was little care taken in the backyard space, and her lawn was not grass but mostly mud for years. Disgusting. After a time, some attempt at a lawn was made, but it was allowed to grow long, to contain too many weeds, and I was glad when a tall fence was placed between us. We rarely communicated except when necessary. She prattled on and on during those times, and I had to eventually cut her off and retreat into myself. Neighbors. Unnecessary. Unhelpful. Unuseful.

Additional houses were built along the block, but we rarely communicated. On the corner next to my dull north neighbor was a building whose bottom floor was some kind of shop. Various small apartments were located on the top two floors. Rather common. A sidewalk separated me from the Boulevard and parkway across the street. It was kept up by the city for years. Lately, the care of it has been haphazard at best. Weeds have been allowed to proliferate along the curbs, and garbage is sometimes seen overflowing the wire cans which the city has placed there. They are chained to either a tree or one of the water-fountains which generally do not work. Such a shame. Since the city has extended miles south and west, it seems too large to care for correctly. Believe me, it was not always this way. In the early days, there was pride.

There it is…the neighborhood and my place in it. I suspect you are surprised at my ability to recall all these events and facts, but it is not just some that I recollect. I know everything that happens in my sphere. I can name and describe every human who spent any time in me, including those who were just visitors as well as long-time residents. I am able to conjure up each and every conversation held in any of my rooms, including my back lawn and garage area, on my sturdy cement front porch, the front sidewalk, both side walkways. I know the cries of joy and ecstasy, the sobs of disappointment and anger, the yelps of pain and surprise. I can recite them all, can review the lives which were lived in me, can tell story after story about the humans on my main floor, the upstairs rooms, the garden apartment, can recite word for word what secrets I know, am able to shame and laugh and commiserate with the humans who spent time in my red-brick walls. I can repeat it all, if I wish. But I don't. Humans are not worth the trouble. Their stories are basic. They are boring. Live, love, laugh…blah, blah, blah. They all end identically. Humans die. Such repetition is numbing. If I could rid my walls and wood and bricks of all the nonsense I have heard, I would. It is not possible. It is not safe for me to do so. Words and emotions and stories are stuffed into my brick being and cannot be disposed. So, I shuffle them around, moving them back into the red oxide bricks until they are scrunched up into each other, overlapping language and dialects and sounds, but I will not, cannot, allow them to escape. They are part of what makes me so strong. Human stories: engorged in my bricks.

This recitation could end now. I could stop. I have considered it. The humans who lived in me are not memorable. Neither are their stories. Except for a few. Less than a half dozen. I release these stories periodically and allow them to shift and swirl around me because of what transpired. Those few humans left something of their lives in me. I mean that literally. There are five secrets hidden in me, in my space. I don't think they will ever be discovered. Some have been hidden for decades. These are the stories I will recount. The only ones. The humans involved are all gone now. I don't miss them, but their stuff is left here, like a popcorn hull which can't seem to be removed from a set of human teeth. Aggravating, annoying, agonizing.

So, I will recall those stories. Offer them as part of my own. Offer them without comment, or at least as little as possible because I am not a judge. I am not a jury. I am an observer. I am an onlooker. I am a witness. I am a viewer, a watcher.

I am a recipient of all deeds.
I am an inheritor of all words.
I am a keeper of all secrets.

I am.

2

Original Residents, 1889

Frankly, I don't want to mention names of the dozens of people who resided in me with the exception of the few who stories and secrets I will recount. But I will provide a listing of the first group: the ones who were initially responsible for my essence. There are two reasons for this. First, they are involved with the initial two tales I intend to narrate. There is no getting around that, and to avoid unnecessary and lengthy explanations, I will review, briefly as possible, their relationships with each other. The second reason I need to explain, again, as briefly as possible, is because their lives affected my innards, specifically, the changes in the upstairs rooms. Don't worry. This will all become clear. I have no intention of burdening readers with lots of names to remember, so I will only refer to their relationships to each other. They aren't that important anyway. The first residents were:

Husband #1

Now this needs clarification. There will be a Husband #2 in this list. Both are important to my story, but #1 was the human who not only helped create me, but was the brick mason who monitored the other bricklayers and who, oh so carefully and with his own hands, placed the red face-bricks of which, could I express emotions, I would be justly proud. He supervised the other workers because he was their leader and organizer. If I were able to be fond of any humans, I would be fond of him. In fact, I come so close to being fond, that I will use his, and only his, name. It was Walter. He was an excellent brick mason. His mortar was perfectly thick and carefully measured; he worked quickly and was able to regularly lay five hundred bricks a day (only the best can do that), and the bricks were level and evenly set. His mortar was well-mixed, precise, sound, and the fact that he died while laying bricks at another house, falling when he was up high on some unsteady scaffolding, would have broken my heart, if I had one. His death caused Husband #2 to enter the family. Eventually, #2 brought his older sister with him who…but I don't want to get ahead of the story.

Back to the list:

Walter (Husband #1)
Wife
Wife's mother (Grandmother or *Babcia*)
Son
Daughter
Husband #2
Older Sister
Housemaid #1
Housemaid #2 (Different maids. Different times.)

I was mostly ready for the first set of humans in the spring of 1889, and that is when Walter and his family moved in.

At first, it was just Walter, the wife, son, and daughter. The best thing about those children was that they were not very young. They were at that in-between stage: not screaming and crying creatures, not adults. The daughter was eleven and the son thirteen. They moved in with what furniture they had, set a few things in place, and began to organize their additional possessions. Although my exterior was actualized, there were interior tasks which required completion, and slowly, too slowly for my tastes, they were finished. The bedrooms on the first and second floors needed painting; the bathroom upstairs needed minor plumbing completed; the shelving in the pantry was not set, and foodstuffs, pots, and various cooking implements were set randomly wherever there was a space. Late nights and long weekends were needed to organize and complete the multitude of tasks. When it was finally done, when everything was painted and decorated and placed, the wife's mother, *Babcia* (Grandma) moved in.

Babcia settled into the first bedroom off the front parlor, and shoved as much of her own furniture as she could into the room. Periodic snuffling sounds were heard coming from her because she missed the items she had to sell: a piano, a large dining room table and chairs, two rocking chairs, a number of additional smaller belongings. Now, I am unsure why any human would need three rocking chairs. Yes, three. She sold two and kept one. She had Walter drag the thing into the house and put it in the parlor next to the fireplace. She would sit and rock and crochet and hum some sort of tune she said was one her own mother had hummed years ago when she lived in the *old country*.

Babcia wasn't a terrible bother, and she did much of the cooking and baking until Housemaid #1 was hired. The baking I did not mind. I have no olfactory sense, but smells produce their own set of colors and sounds. The smell/sounds of cinnamon and yeast and vanilla and sweet fruits and spices offered welcomed tones and hues. Wholesome pastels, graciously tinkled and wound their way into the walls where other words and sounds made space for them. It was the cabbage dishes, the *Kapusta* and *Haluski*, the Polish sausages and *Kielbasa* whose smacking pungency can still be discovered were I to allow them to escape. They crinkled and crimped and crushed in colors of brown and gray and a mustardy yellow, and mashed against the kitchen walls, mushing their way into the plaster, finding spaces as the other actual spoken words and sounds squirmed together, avoiding them. Garlic and onions! Please! When Housemaid #1 was hired, she was a gentler cook, making softer meals whose fumes did not attack one's olfactory sense in the way Babcia's culinary attempts did. Walter and the rest of the family seemed to enjoyed the gentler meals, and it was just Babcia who complained. Whenever Housekeeper #1 was absent or had days off, the kitchen was ruled by Babcia, and the zing of cabbage and garlic and onion, used in abundance, would again, hit the air with their savage aromas.

Babcia's compensation from the sale of her extra belongings helped to replace the old wood cookstove which was used at first. Once money was available, the wife and Babcia poured through a catalogue from the Chicago Stove and Range Company (Located on East 26th Street in what I understood from my neighbor to the north, was another red-brick building, quite a large and spacious warehouse, although the brick was not as newly sparkling as mine.) and ordered a new cookstove. It took some time before it could be delivered, and everyone needed to learn how to light the stove, adjust the damper, arrange the pots properly on the cooktop. The new cookstove used both wood and coal, but eventually a gas line was run to the house and a gas stove put in place. That was years later, long after Babcia was gone and no longer making the Kapusta.

The son and daughter moved into the upstairs rooms, each taking one of the rooms after arguing about who should have which. I take back the comment about older children not screaming and crying. They eventually settled the argument, and the son took the larger of the two rooms, the one with the built-in bookcases, and the daughter had the smaller room. She pushed and pulled and finally moved her heavy dresser against the door which connects the two rooms, blocking the son out, keeping him from entering and scaring her by jumping on her bed early in the mornings. Mostly, they got along. The main argument centered around the upstairs bathroom and its use. The son was attempting to grow a moustache, and he did spend an inordinate amount of time glaring in the mirror at the spots he was convinced hairs were sprouting. At first, there was no bathtub upstairs. One was put in later (Husband #2 saw to this.), so the downstairs bathtub was shared by the entire family. There were five of them, and then Housemaid #1, once she moved in, increased the number to six. Each one took a night to bathe, a time when the claw-footed bathtub and bathroom became a private chamber strictly for one, and it seemed to work out. There were, at first, a few disagreements about the nights, and on rare occasions, for one reason or another, one member of the household would ask another to change nights. The rule was that each human was to clean the space after their time in it. They managed to abide by this, although the son rarely completed the job thoroughly, and his sloppiness created loud disagreements between him and the daughter whose night was after his. Those loud and spiteful spats are shoved well back into these walls. I never wish to hear that again.

So, Housemaid #1. For the first year Walter and his family, just the five of them, were the ones living in me. Walter worked six days a week, often nine or more hours a day, and then came home and worked on me, completing unfinished tasks or making necessary repairs. At times, he helped a friend build his own house. That was the way it was done. The humans assisted each other in building houses because that was the only way to afford one. Work was done at nights until it was too dark to see, and Sunday afternoons were given to the building tasks. I must admit, it seemed a hard life. But there was always a party when a family moved into the new house, and all the humans appeared happy then. The wife worked too. She was a seamstress, and once everything was completed in the house, she set up her sewing machine at the south end of the dining room, spread her sewing tools along the built-in sideboard, and began to take in work again. The money she brought in was helpful, but the housekeeping and cooking suffered.

Babcia was moved in to help with the cooking and upkeep, and for a time, it all went smoothly. But Babcia kept forgetting to do things. She would forget to put the correct numbered sign in the back window for the iceman, and he wouldn't deliver the needed blocks of ice. She had trouble with the new cookstove and burned a number of meals and ruined two perfectly good pots. She would yell at the son and daughter, the son especially, and they would disappear into their bedrooms. A few minutes later she would have forgotten about whatever the issue was and want them to sit with her, keeping her company on the porch and was upset when they refused. But when she burned her hand so badly on the cookstove that a costly doctor visit was necessary, Walter and the wife decided that it was time to get some additional help. The wife was making money with her work; she didn't have much time to complete house tasks. Enter: Housemaid #1.

This woman was somewhere in age between the wife and Babcia although she was closer to the wife in years. She had been with another family for a long time, but when they moved to a place called Milwaukee, she was forced to move in with her brother and his wife, and the two women did not get along. This was the explanation given to Walter's wife. I must comment here about the human behavior I've seen. What is going on? Why is it not possible for all of that species to behave, well, charitably? Really. The fights and arguments and meanness I have stored in my walls and bricks take up so much room that I created a special spot for those words and emotions in each space where they have occurred. It is near the floor. Compressed into the recess. Crowded into each other. Occasionally, I can hear them shoving and pushing each other around and when it gets too loud for me, I need to quiet them. I warn them that, should I need to, I can release them all into the air where they will dissipate rapidly. This usually works, at least for a while. They don't know that I cannot actually do this, but mendacity is a trick learned from the humans who, I suppose, are good for something. Back to Housemaid #1. At first, she came to work only during the days, but when Babcia stopped doing even the minimal amount of cleaning and bad cooking, a deal was struck. For a reduced amount of pay and a day off weekly, she could move into the room off the kitchen, the small one meant for a maid, and the room became part of her recompense. That worked out. Apparently, she and her brother's wife constantly argued, and having her own room in the house where she worked, not having to trudge back and forth across many muddy streets to a distant house, having a kitchen with decent pots and pans and a new cookstove, was a reasonable exchange. Housemaid #1 stayed for a number of years. When her brother's wife died, she decided to move back in with him. Anyway, by that time, she and Husband #2 were not getting along. Story to come.

Walter and his son had disagreements. The son graduated from elementary school and then started high school because Walter thought an education was important. He didn't want the son to follow in his footsteps and work the long hours he did. He believed a high school diploma would allow his son to get a job in an office or a bank, allow him to wear a suit and tie to work rather than overalls, help him find a decent Catholic girl who was a good cook, marry, and make a better life for himself. The American Dream. He told this to the son on a weekly basis, and, on a weekly basis, was disappointed in the boy. The son disliked school. He went most days, but once he got a job at a nearby store sweeping the floors, stocking the shelves, washing the windows, earning a small amount of money, he yearned to quit school and work full-time. He was required to hand over his meager pay to Walter, and he did. Well, most of it. He pocketed some pennies for himself, using them to purchase small things he wanted: candy, new combs, a bowtie he saw for sale in a ready-made clothing shop which he told the daughter would look snazzy when he wore it. But most of his coins were stored away in the hopes that eventually, he could purchase the thing he wanted most: a bicycle. He had a plan. With a bicycle, he could obtain a job delivering telegrams. He would wear a blue uniform coat which had bright buttons on it and travel throughout the city, speeding along the streets, waving to the schmucks who were walking to school, wasting their time learning nonsense while he was earning real bucks. This is what I heard him say as he talked out loud to himself up in that first bedroom, his words lifting to the ceiling, anxious and proud, colored with the bright blue of the desired uniform, pulsing with youthful energy. He counted the pennies and nickels he hid in a sock and placed against the back of his bottom dresser drawer. The son worked at the store, gave a half-hearted attempt at schoolwork, and continued to save his pennies. When he turned sixteen, disaster struck the household in the form of a poorly built, wobbly scaffold set up over an extremely high building being created in the Downtown Chicago area. The father, Walter, was on it, completing the laying of bricks, a job in which he excelled, and as he reached over for additional mortar, the scaffolding collapsed. He fell to the ground, splitting open his head on a pile of common yellow bricks. This was the story I heard when the police arrived to give the family the awful news. I watched the words quake and quiver in grief, easing themselves in wretchedness into the ceiling. I never understood this death stuff. My walls and bricks have a special place (I group similar sounds and words together.) for the sobs and cries and dins caused by such agonies. And Walter's death caused many.

There will be no lengthy report, no heartfelt narration, no cordial summary of the time afterwards, of the wake held in my parlor, of the removal of the casket out the front bay window because it could not turn through the door, of the procession down my cement steps and to the street where the wagon hauled it to the church, of the repast which was later held throughout my rooms where too much beer was spilled on my floors, and my inside space was laden with the odor of onions and garlic, cabbage and sausage, fried pork and roasted potatoes for days afterwards. Walter. He fell; he died; he was buried. Humans. I remain amazed at their typical, and frankly, stupid ends. I watched as neighbors, fellow workers, friends, distant relatives came to mourn him, to offer their condolences to the grieving family, to partake of the food and drink which neighboring friends and church women brought in. And as the group of people gathered to talk and mourn and eat and drink, I noticed *that man*. He walked through me, taking note of my parlor's coving and ornamental plasterwork, running his hands along my staircases, glancing into the bedrooms whose doors he pushed open with the toe of his boot, spending time at the bookcases and dining room sideboard, examining the contents of each. He examined me carefully, and I could almost hear the thoughts in his head. If the noise throughout my rooms had not been so blaringly loud, I could have listened in.

I recognized him. He was one of the carpenters who had helped to build me, and he was interested in the woodwork because he helped to create it. I know from overheard conversations that he belonged to some of the newer workers' organizations such as the Knights of Labor and the United Brotherhood of Carpenters. Neither organization was particularly successful, and while their goals were lofty, some work strikes had been called, and I heard from both the Boulevard and the cinder alley that there was violence in the streets due to their demands. He took part. I am not judging. Humans have been unfair to each other, fighting with each other for longer than I've been around. But this man, this worker had a certain gleam in his eye as he walked around, shaking many hands and expressing his sorrow at the loss of a man he called "friend". As he stalked through my space, his eyes were constantly moving over the furniture, the knick-knacks, the kitchen appliances, my walls and floors. He was particularly kind to the wife, holding her two hands in his, bending down to where she was seated, looking into her face, placing his hand on her shoulder as she wiped her eyes, glancing at her throughout his time in the crowded space. Before he left, and he was one of the last to do so, he made sure to tell the wife that he understood her pain, being a widower himself, that he could be called on to help whenever she needed it, that his sorrow was almost as great as hers, that Walter had been a *prince of a fellow*, that he would miss him. I listened as he spoke, as his artful words, tinged with a hint of misleading invention strutted to the ceilings, placing themselves into a cluster, staring with barely concealed distain at the other words which were already there. I knew what this human was about. He was vying for a new job. He wanted to be Husband #2.

3
Husband #2

Time means nothing to me. It's a human construct, created in an attempt to have control over nature and other humans. As if they could. However, I have become used to noting time in human terms, and the years after Walter's death brought changes. Many changes, in fact.

The first change was with the son. He was sixteen in human years, and Walter's death meant he had become *the man of the family*. Those words, always bold and strutting, marching to the walls, pushing, carefully but sternly, other words out of the way, were used multiple times during the wake and funeral. Friends, fellow workers, neighbors would come up to him, shake his hand, sometimes offer a manly hug and tell him that. They would explain to him what he had, due to a shaky and ill built scaffold, become. Silly words, but he came to believe them. The son had grown tall and was able to look directly into the faces of the men who apprised him of that fact, although in a few cases, they looked up at him. He mulled the words over, waited some time, and then went to the wife, his mother, and said to her, "I'm now *the man of the family*, and I need to help provide for everyone. I'm quitting school and working full time. I've already talked to my boss. He said I could start full-time at the store in two weeks because he is losing the clerk who is there." The wife was shocked, and she argued weakly and without much conviction for a time, but then gave in. She saw the sense in this. They needed the money.

The son was given Walter's old suit to wear. The wife fitted it to him, cutting and sewing it to adjust to his thinner frame, and when he came down the stairs that first day, ready to work as a full-time clerk, he was dressed in the suit and had on the bowtie he purchased, the one he thought he'd looked snazzy wearing. When the wife saw him, she burst into tears. It wasn't what he expected, and tears clouded his eyes too. Were I able to produce feelings, I might have felt the emotions they conveyed: sorrow, pride, anguish, fear, anxiety, confusion. I saw all these sensations lifting away from them both, climbing into the air, pushing against the ceiling; they were so strong. But I simply noted them, and after the son left for his job and the wife wiped her eyes again and went on with her chores, I corralled them into a wall near one of the plaster roses in the coving of the parlor. They were shy and uncomfortable with each other, but I knew they belonged together. There they stayed. They are still there.

The son didn't graduate from high school and wear a suit to work at a bank or office, but he started out in one. His new position, he discovered, included not only his previous tasks of cleaning, sweeping, and stocking, but also the additional work of carrying, counting, and smiling. He did not like the new job and complained nightly to the daughter about it. He said nothing to his mother. He did not want to upset her. He worked for the store until it was sold, and by that time, he was married and needed additional funds to help support the baby he and his spouse were expecting, so he got a different job. He put on a pair of overalls, went to work at one of the manufacturing plants along Pershing Road, earned more money, and grew up to look like Walter. I didn't see him much after he left. Sometimes he would stop by to see his mother, and sometimes he would bring his family to visit. Once he moved out, he didn't want to be around much. I understood it wasn't me. It was the carpenter. The son didn't like him. The carpenter became Husband #2. Another change.

The carpenter took his time courting the wife. He figured she needed to mourn for a while. He was correct. I watched as he slowly insinuated himself into her life. After the funeral, he let some weeks pass. Then, one Sunday afternoon, I viewed him walking slowly past me, glancing at my porch, stopping briefly, pretending to look for something in his pocket. No one was outside, and he went on. He must have walked around a street or two before circling back. The third time he came by, the wife was seated on the porch enjoying the afternoon. He stopped and looked quizzically at her, acting surprised to see her seated on her own porch. He smiled, pretending as if he just remembered who she was, walked to the bottom of the steps, lifted his hat, and greeted her.

"Good afternoon. Nice day today. I live a few streets from here and thought I'd take a stroll in the neighborhood. How are you?"

The wife looked at him for a few seconds, trying to remember him, then smiled, and nodded. "Hello. I am fine, and it is a nice day. It's good to see you again."

This conversation, words appearing straight, solid, symmetrical, went on in this vein for a few minutes, and then the carpenter put his hat back on, wished the wife a good day, said that he'd see her again sometime, and left. He was smart, that one. He didn't stay long or push himself on her, but just set the stage for his next move. Two weeks later, again on a Sunday, he showed up at the house. This time, he walked up my stairs and knocked loudly on my front door. He held a package in his arms. When housemaid #1 opened the door, he politely asked if the wife was in because he wished to speak to her. After a short time, the wife appeared at the door and stood patiently while he explained that he had received some pork from a friend, and it was too much for him to use, being a widower and all, and he thought he would drop a portion of it off for the wife and her family. It was good and would make a fine stew. And so, the visits began.

He didn't come every Sunday. Sometimes, on a late weekday evening, before the sun was completely gone, he climbed my front steps, always holding some package. The story was generally the same; his words were always gracious, but I noticed their slight air of artifice. He was just thinking about the family and saw the butcher had a sale on sausage. He picked some up for them and for himself, although he didn't need much, living alone as he did. The canned goods which he offered might come in handy. Besides, he had bought too much, forgetting, for a second, he was a widower. There were two new brooms given to him by an old friend, and he only needed one; couldn't the housemaid use a new one? He had no housemaid and did his own sweeping, being alone. These were some late summer flowers the neighbor woman gave to him from her garden, and he thought they would brighten the dining room table in Walter's house. He kept a few for himself, but wasn't sure exactly how to arrange them since his late wife had assumed that task. I am pretty sure it was the flowers which got him the invitation for Sunday lunch. He happily accepted, and the Sunday lunches with the family, and this old friend of poor dead Walter's, began. I had to admire the timing of this carpenter. It was precise. He was patient. His words left his lips and smoothly and theatrically slid up to the ceiling, cozying next to the wife's answers. It was months before he was invited in. But his persistence paid off. It took a little over a year of Sunday lunches and periodic Wednesday night suppers, of packages of pork and sausages, of bags of extra canned goods, of delicious bakery sweets (I assume from the bakery I heard was located along 35th Street in a new yellow-brick building.), of a new extra shovel for the winter, and the marriage deal was made. He would sell his small cottage some streets away, move his furniture in, store it in the empty basement. On a Saturday morning, one month after a Memorial Mass for Walter was said at St. Mary's Catholic Church, the carpenter and the wife took their vows of marriage to each other at that same church. He became Husband #2. The only problem was the son, who being seventeen at the time this marriage took place, resented being displaced as *the man of the family*.

Everyone else thought the marriage was a solid decision. The daughter, who was an empty-headed fifteen-year-old high schooler, was basically concerned about herself. If this man married her mother, it was fine. After all, the carpenter had periodically given her some ribbons for her hair, and he always seemed to have a small bag of the peppermints she liked. It was enough. Babcia didn't seem to care either. She had lived through two husbands herself, and because both her eyesight and her mind were fading, she sometimes called the carpenter *Walter*. She would smile as he placed a blanket over her lap or got up to retrieve her shawl, and when she turned to him, smiled, and said, "*Dziekuje*, Walter," he smiled back and turned to the wife and gave a slight shoulder shrug meaning *Don't worry, I understand*. Housekeeper #1 had nothing to say about the marriage. She understood that remarriages were usual, and a year was a lengthy time to have no man in the household. She discounted the son and ignored his moods. He was still a child and did not understand adult decisions yet. Besides, she was expecting to receive her full salary again once this carpenter moved in bringing his own pay with him. She had voluntarily taken less money after Walter's death because she understood the problems of being a widow; besides, the wife tearfully asked her to stay despite the lack of funds to pay her. Once she found someone to marry, the wife confided to her that money would not be such an issue, and the housemaid would once again receive her usual amount. Obviously, the carpenter was not the only one planning for a future. The remainder of the neighborhood, their friends, the rest of the workers, even the priest who married them believed this union was for the best. A common practice. But the son was not happy.

The carpenter wasn't mean or cruel to the son. He understood his feelings. He himself had a son from his first marriage who was grown, married, and lived in the neighboring state of Indiana, so he was familiar with the male psyche. He tried to be kind, to engage the son, to bond with him with coaxing and cajoling words and phrases, all of them spoken with just a hint of crooked charm. It was no use. Even when the son answered, it was with restrained anger, the words struggling, needing to be held back by older words. The son's words were anxious to attack, to push, to pinch husband #2's words, and they settled into opposite corners, glowering and side-eyeing each other. On those Wednesdays when the son came home from work and the table was set with an extra plate, he would go into the kitchen, grab a bowl of whatever was being served, and disappear up the back staircase into his room. He would come down the next morning bringing the empty bowl with him. On Sundays, he would fill his plate at the table, then take it, moving into the kitchen to stand and eat at the sink. When he was done, he would place the dish into the sink and walk out the back door to meet up with some friends or visit the young woman he was seeing. He would not return until much later, after the carpenter had gone, and he refused to talk to the wife about this. He was being usurped. He had been told that *he* was *the man of the family*. He was hurt and angry. One Sunday, just as he was placing his empty plate into the sink, he felt a hand on his shoulder and heard his name being called. He turned around to face the carpenter. They were the same height. They were equal in the son's mind.

"Listen, son," started the carpenter, "I know that you…"

The son didn't allow the carpenter to finish the thought. He angrily shrugged his shoulder, and the other man's hand fell from it. He took a step back, speaking in what he considered a virile tone, looked into the usurper's face and said, "I am not your son. I will never be your son. You are not needed here, but you have weaseled your way in. My mother may be fooled, but I am not. Don't speak to me. I have no intentions of talking to you," and the son turned and left the house. He did not return until early the following day, having spent the night at a friend's house. At least that's what he told his weeping mother when he returned to bathe and dress for work.

More change involving human sadness came. Babcia died. The wake, the funeral, the luncheon, all were held only two years after Walter's, and while it was not as crowded, Babcia's friends were there, comforting the wife, talking about her mother, reviewing the unexpected death in detail. Babcia had a friend who lived three houses down the street (I could just see the house which was created with *all* poorly made imported brick. Sad.) and whenever the weather permitted, they would walk to St. Mary's to attend early Friday Mass. Babcia left the house that last day. She had been feeling light-headed for a few days, leaning against my walls until she was steady, but she immediately forgot the feeling once she regained her balance. She did not consider it was anything important. She went down my cement steps very carefully, standing at the bottom to straighten her back and take a breath. I saw her walk the few steps to her friend's house, stop in front, and immediately crumple to the ground. Dead. At least she did not suffer, is what her friends recounted. Whatever that meant. Anyway, Babcia was gone, and the main mourners at the funeral were the wife and husband #2. The son did show up to the wake, but sat in my parlor's far corner looking like a usurped *man of the family*. Really, I will never understand human posturing.

Death was a constant, although the next one did not affect the family personally. The sister-in-law of housemaid #1 died. Her brother wanted her to come back and help raise the last child left to him. She discussed this with the wife, telling her she would stay but needed to receive her initial pay again since Husband #2 had never reinstated her original salary, even though the wife had said it would happen. There was a long discussion between the wife and husband #2 and the words became darker and larger as they spoke. Then there was another discussion. Then one more. (All those conversations are locked into the woodwork where the actual words alternate between reliving their part in the discussions and producing a stony, angry silence. I prefer the silence.) The final outcome was that the wife insisted husband #2 tell housemaid #1 himself that her pay would not be reinstated to the original amount. That conversation was short, the words squirreling their way into the woodwork, puffs of angry smoke evaporating into the ceiling. Housemaid #1 left the following day and returned to her brother's house. Gone.

For a week there was no housemaid, and then additional changes occurred. A new maid was hired. She was younger and more alert than the first one, and while she was not as good a cook, there were few complaints. Husband #2 was content with her because she was willing to accept the same lower wages that made Housemaid #1 leave. The wife was busy with her own sewing and work, and as long as the house was cleaned and the meals made, she didn't complain either. The daughter didn't care. She continued high school and, as often as possible, visited her best friend who had an older brother with whom the daughter was enchanted. And the son, well, he left when he turned eighteen. I heard he shared a room with a friend, continued to work, and eventually married the girl he had been courting. I wish he had been able to take his angry words and noxious thoughts with him, but they remained. I keep them sequestered in the wall behind the built-in bookcases in his room and would never allow them to venture out again. There were so many of them that they strengthened the wall behind the cases. At least they were good for something. For a while (One year? Two years?) a serenity of sorts eased into me. When the daughter graduated high school, her mother insisted on hosting a celebration during which the engagement between the daughter and her friend's brother was announced. The two married and moved into their own small apartment some streets away.

The son was gone. The daughter was gone. Babcia was gone. Walter was long gone. My upstairs was empty. I watched as husband #2 periodically climbed the stairs, looked around my rooms on the second floor and nodded his head. "Hmm," he would drone again and again, and his quizzical sounds floated up to the ceiling where they would melt into the corners and spread out like the salted lard husband #2 generously spread on his rye bread. More changes were coming.

4

More Changes

I seemed empty to the wife and husband #2. I suppose it was because just the two of them and housemaid #2 were living in me. Housemaid #2 was not the talker housemaid #1 had been and consequently, not much company for the wife. The new housemaid was younger and had made friends with some of the other hired helpers on the street, and while she worked cleaning and washing and cooking throughout the day, often at night she would visit with one of her neighborhood friends, leaving the wife alone. Husband #2 was busy several nights a week with his workers organization meetings, and the son stayed away while the daughter rarely visited, so the wife was by herself. She complained continually to husband #2 until he finally came up with a suggestion.

"My older sister's husband died last fall, and she is alone. If she moves into Babcia's old room, she would be company for you. Anyway, she wants to sell the farm because she cannot work it by herself. What do you think?"

The wife hesitated. Husband #2 had two sisters, and she had met the younger one. That sister had come to dinner a couple times, bringing her own husband once and her youngest daughter the second time, and the wife barely tolerated her. The sister was loud, opinionated, and impolite. She complained about the toughness of the meat, the saltiness of the potatoes, the lack of sweetness in the cake, all of which the wife had helped to make. The sister drank too many beers, and she allowed a very loud burp to escape during the last sip as she laughed. The wife was appalled, and frankly, that burp is still in the upper part of the dining room. You would think that over the years, its sound would have faded, but it hasn't. The wife was hesitant about allowing the older sister, the one she hadn't met, to live with them. What if she is just like the younger one?

Husband #2 saw the look on the wife's face, and proceeded to assure her. "This sister is not like my younger one. She was a teacher in a country school and married a bachelor farmer in the town. They never had children, and I know that since he died, the farm life has been difficult for her. I think the two of you will get along, but why don't I invite her for a visit, and you can decide for yourself?"

The wife hesitantly agreed. The sister came up the following month. To everyone's surprise and relief, the wife and the sister rapidly eased into a friendship with each other. After only three days, the wife herself, suggested that the sister move into the house, and the older woman was delighted with the invitation. It was decided that, for a time, husband #2 would stay with his sister at her small farm, to help her with the sale of it, the disposal of many items, the moving of certain possessions to Chicago. In the meanwhile, housemaid #2 and the wife cleaned Babcia's room, moving their furniture and washing my walls. Some of Babcia's belongings were found, and the wife cried for part of a day with remembrance, but stopped crying when she found an old hat which contained hidden cash. Twenty-five dollars in all, and she bribed housemaid #2 with some of it so that she would not tell husband #2. They laughed; tears forgotten. I watched the teary cries and the delighted laughter intermingle as they rose to the ceiling where they could not be separated. The room was readied.

The sister moved in. She brought some of her own furniture with her and everything was reorganized and set into place. Because she had been a teacher, (I admit, not ever having a need to learn anything, I didn't understand that human occupation. Carpenter, brick layer, cook, seamstress: those I saw a need for, but a teacher?) she brought many books with her, placing them in stacks around the bedroom because there was no other place for them. When the wife saw this, she went to husband #2 and gave him a task.

"You are her brother and a carpenter. Why don't you make a bookcase for those books? She is bound to trip over them at some point. Did you see how many she brought with her?"

There were certainly many books. The sister would reread one of them nightly as she sat with the wife who worked on the hand-sewing which needed to be completed. Sometimes she would read aloud from one of them, the words arching and stretching to the woodwork, easing in together, forming small precise paragraphs, and the wife enjoyed this. Husband #2 built a large bookcase which he sanded, stained, polished, and with the help of a friend, brought from the basement to the bedroom and anchored it against a wall. The sister was delighted and spent the following day organizing and reorganizing the books, moving them into place until they were exactly as she wanted them. It was a pleasure to hear the sister's soft voice as she spoke to her books saying things like "Oh, I will need to reread you again," and "I have forgotten about you. There, don't you look splendid in that corner!" She did love those books,

and although she offered to let the wife and husband #2 choose any
book they wished to read, neither one took that offer. They were not the
reading sort.

I must admit, the sister was likeable. She was gentle in her
movements and soft with her voice, and I don't think I ever heard a
loud or rude sound from her. She was very different than her younger
sibling. When the older sister spoke, it was enjoyable to watch her words.
She told the wife one evening about the flower garden she had kept at
the small farm. As she spoke of the spring daffodils, the summer snap-
dragons, the fall mums, the words rose about her, forming a wreath just
above her head. They stayed there, swaying in a circle, and when they
found their space in the wall and into an empty brick, they were polite
while entering. There was no pushing or shoving. The larger words
helped the smaller ones find a suitable spot, and they quietly murmured
amongst themselves. I could not smell them, but I believe they gave off
a floral scent which was pleasing. All the sister's words followed this
pattern. When she spoke of the farm animals, the horse and the chickens,
the goats they kept for their milk, the purring house cats who enjoyed
sitting on her lap, I saw those words and they became the various animals
around her, creating tiny animal noises which were never overwhelming.
Her description of the farm and her dead husband's work on it became
a pastoral scene. The school room where she worked teaching children
appeared on a large slate board which erased itself as the words entered
the walls. The vegetables she canned lined up on a tall shelf, and the
herbs she dried hung themselves gently from the cellar ceiling, then
quietly, one glass jar of vegetables, one tidy bunch of herbs at a time
drifted into the wall, settled into the bricks. I enjoyed listening to her
speak with her mild and carefully modulated tones, the pitch and tenor of
her words acting as music in the air. Such pleasure! I am almost tempted
to give you her name, to describe her being, to allow you to admire
her as I did. But I will not. In the end, even this person, this sister, is
only a human. Here for a time; then gone. Soon dead. So, on to a more
important topic: new construction.

Husband #2 visited the empty bedrooms upstairs often. He
looked at the rooms and examined the furniture which was there. The
son had taken nothing with him. The few pieces he used were still in the
room: a chair, a bed, a dresser. The daughter asked for and was given
the things in her room, so that room was empty. The man walked the
hallway, examining the two empty closet spaces and the bathroom. The
bathroom was spacious and as he knocked at the walls and examined
the plumbing which was there, he made a decision. One evening, after

dinner, when housemaid #2, having completed her chores, was visiting a friend, he spoke to the wife and sister.

"I have an idea, a plan to earn additional money. We should become landlords."

This attracted the attention of both women, and the sister put down her book, the wife laid aside her sewing, and they looked at him.

"We do not have the funds to complete the downstairs garden apartment. That will take both time and money, and it is not possible right now. But…" and here he paused for effect, "…there is something we can do now to bring in needed funds. I have examined the empty rooms upstairs, and there is no reason they cannot be rented out. I believe they can be turned into a small apartment, and the money they can bring in will both help us to eventually complete the garden apartment and form a little nest egg for our old age." He paused here, and I suspect he was waiting for applause. The women were silent.

"Well? What do you think?"

The wife spoke first. "I suppose that will work, but I have a number of questions about the plan."

The sister spoke next. "If I can help, I will, but this is not my house. Perhaps we should hear about your plan."

Husband #2 nodded. "What questions are there?"

"Well, for one, the bathroom situation. I'm not sure I want strangers bathing down here, in our bathroom."

"Thought of that. Spoke to some of my plumber friends, and we would need to purchase a bathtub for upstairs. It can be done, and the plumbing would not take too long to do. I even have someone in mind to do it, and because I helped him with making a table and chairs for his house a while ago, he owes me a favor. What else?

The wife sighed. "There is no cookstove up there, and I'm not sure I want one there. How would the renters eat? Again, would they eat with us? What about our privacy? Would they have a key to the house? How could we trust them? Would they keep things clean? Then there is the laundry issue. Their clothes would need to be cleaned, and we don't have enough towels or bed linens, and we would need to put out additional money for all these things, and…"

The husband held up his hand. "Ok, let's take one thing at a time and talk about them. I have some ideas, and between the three of us, we can figure this out," and the conversation continued.

It continued for the following week, and the week after that. The words were often loud, managing to bump into each other causing creaks and cracks, groans and crunches, and at times I needed to usher them up into a corner where they chose sides, periodically emitting low growls. But, at the beginning of the fourth week, conversations having taken place whenever there was time, most issues were decided. Not everything. The humans were aware that their current decisions could be changed once actual renters were present. They knew this would be a new venture for them and that they were, and this was a human phrase I had never heard before: *babes in the woods*. The sister said it, and I watched as those words floated up, forming a picture of a human baby sitting on the floor of a wooded area with trees all around. They disappeared into the corner of the dining room, and the expression on the word-baby's face made me think it was going to cry. I must admit that I enjoyed listening to the sister speak.

The needed work was accomplished. The bathtub was moved in and plumbing completed in the upstairs bathroom. Necessary furniture, most of it belonging to husband #2, was moved from my basement to the rooms: a table and three chairs, an old easy chair, a side table. The bedroom was set up with a large bed, a dresser, a bedside table. A rug was placed on each room's floor once the floors were washed and polished. Two old pictures were hung on the walls. Things were set in place; everything was cleaned. Windows shined. Draperies hung. A visit to the dry goods store was made and towels and simple white bed linens were sewed. Everything was readied.

They checked the newspapers for apartment advertisements, deciding what to write in theirs, determining how much to charge. This took a long time. The sister was helpful in completing the ad, and when it was finished and all were somewhat satisfied with it, a copy was sent to the daily morning paper, the husband hung copies in the Knights of Labor and United Brotherhood of Carpenters meeting rooms, the wife went to the corner store and asked to place a sign in their window, and the sister created a large and perfectly written placard to place in the front bay window which read:

To Let:

Lovely apartment with private bath:

Inquire Within

And then they waited.

(Be patient, reader, I am looking for the words of the advertisement. I want to make sure I obtain the correct one because there were quite a number of changes made before they all agreed about them and ALL were read aloud many times. Hold on…There…I found them deep behind that wall. This is the version they used):

Reasonable and clean!

Apartment to Let

Private bath

Short term lease available (1 to 3 months)
Long term lease available (6 months to a year)
Partial Board available (Daily breakfast and Sunday lunch)
Or Full Board (Daily breakfast, Daily dinner, Sunday lunch)
Close to shops, restaurants, Chinese laundry, Barber shop

Clean and serious renters only.

The address was given at the end, and once potential renters were interviewed, the apartment rules were handed to them. If there were issues with any of them, if the renters questioned the reason for one, or argued about something, they were politely shown the door. The rules were:

No cooking, drinking, smoking, spitting in apartment.
Rent due the 10th of each month. First month in advance.
Fresh towels and bed linens every Thursday.
Daily breakfast: oats, coffee, toast. Eggs on Saturday.
Dinners: House meals.
Politeness and honesty expected.

That last rule was added by the sister. She said that when she taught, that was a rule in her classroom, and she believed it was important. As it turned out, it was easier to enforce in a classroom. They became landlords.

5

Landlords

Of course it was not easy. There were arguments and problems, issues undecided, financial troubles and setbacks, words and emotions flying through my space, assertive, aggressive, arrogant, barely controllable. And all this happened before anyone even moved in. The family met with disputes and obstructions. The first issue was with housemaid #2. She was unhappy with the extra work she assumed would be hers. I know the exact words she used.

"Well, if I am to take over the cleaning of the upstairs, the cooking and dishes and laundry for extra people in this house, I am going to need more compensation. After all, I am kept busy from daybreak until nightfall with just the family, and that was *all* I was hired to care for," and those jingling, shrill words lifted up to the ceiling and refused to enter anywhere for a long time. They hung around to see what else would be joining them.

The wife answered, "Yes, I know, but we are not sure what is going to happen. I understand your position. I promise that when my husband comes home, we will talk about it."

"Fine. But I am leaving as soon as I finish the dishes to visit with a friend. I don't need to be around when this discussion takes place. By the way, we are almost out of onions and potatoes," and housemaid #2 stood with her hand on her hips, her words hovering just below the last ones.

"I'll add them to the list," and the wife left to go back to her sewing.

I believe it necessary to correct the housemaid's claim that she was *busy from daybreak to nightfall.* No. There were plenty of times she hung over the back fence talking to the housemaid next door or stood in the alleyway gossiping with a group who would meet there on a regular basis, pretending to work at outside tasks. I know. I observed it all. I could see her completing her tasks. I didn't care that she took shortcuts with the cooking and baking or didn't clean the icebox as regularly as necessary. But I was not happy when she didn't wipe up my kitchen floors as often as she should have and left the cooking splotches from her messy meal-making on my walls until she needed to take a butter knife and pry the bits off. Really, I should not be treated so harshly. If I could have done something about it all, I would have. Sometimes being incorporeal is frustrating.

The discussion that evening was a lengthy one, and nothing was decided. Husband #2 did not want to increase the housemaid's salary, but the wife thought the woman had a point. There was nothing decided that night. Nor the following one or the night after that. The discussions were often heated, the words lifting from lips, hanging around just above heads, disorderly, disarrayed, disjointed. The sister excused herself and shut her bedroom door so that she would not need to hear what was becoming a nightly argument. Finally, the wife drew the sister into the discussion and asked her for an opinion.

"Well, I do not want to get into the midst of this, but I think I might have an idea," said the sister as the others listened. "The housemaid should be paid some additional money for the additional work she will do, and you should decide the amount, but I will offer myself as a…" and here she stopped to think, "…manager, if you can think of it like that, for the rented space. I worked hard on the farm. I helped my husband take care of the animals, and worked at my flower and vegetable gardens…" (I heard a soft mooing of the sequestered *wordcows* as she spoke.), "and I cleaned and kept the house. You have both been kind to ask me here, and I don't mind doing additional work. I am adept at it, and if I take over a weekly cleaning, and the housemaid is given a small increase for the additional cooking and dish washing, she might be satisfied. I could keep the books and account for the money spent. What do you think?"

Husband #2 and the wife looked at each other and they both shrugged. "That sounds reasonable," said the wife, "but what about laundry?"

The husband raised his hands and said, "Well, the advertisement does claim we are close to a Chinese laundry, and there are two within walking distance. The renter should be responsible for his own laundry service, but the clean towels and sheets will be our responsibility. Is that fair?"

"I can help with the laundering of the towels and linens," said the sister. "I did it all on the farm. If I offer to help the housemaid on Thursdays, and clean the upstairs floor and the bathroom that day, don't you think that will be useful and fair? I can repay you in that way for allowing me to live here with you."

The husband nodded. "Fine. When the housemaid returns, we will talk to her. Now how much extra should we offer her? Anything we give her will cut into whatever profits we make…" and the discussion continued. Again, nothing was decided that evening, and when the housemaid returned, nothing was said. It took additional days until all the details were worked out. When housemaid #2 was informed of the new offer for her additional work, she gave a rare smile and nodded her head and agreed. "That's acceptable." The housemaid skimped on her words and they, tiny and weak, joined her other larger jingling and shrill ones up in the corner where they cowered together, taunted by the stridency of the earlier words. Sigh.

My upstairs was ready to receive renters, but despite the readiness, the sister traveled up the stairs daily to check things out and readjust some of the furnishings. She took down the dusty old pictures husband #2 had hung on the walls and found cheap but colorful replacements. An ancient but serviceable tablecloth was placed on the old table, and even though the windows had been cleaned and washed, the sister scrubbed them with a concoction she said she used at the farm, and the rewashed windows squeaked with freshness. She took the small sign from the window and rewrote the message on a larger piece of cardboard, placing it in the upstairs window where it appeared prominently. And then, there was nothing to do except wait for renters to come.

They eventually came, but it took a while. I am sure my location…in the middle of a quiet street, away from the busy cross streets of Archer to the south and 35th Street to the north…was a factor, but renters did show up. At first, the humans were extremely picky and rejected the potential renters who presented problems. "Too young." "Too messy." "Too untrustworthy looking." Those comments rose up unhappily, appearing twitchy and dithery, and created a mood of fretfulness in the front parlor where all the interviews were held. Finally, they agreed on a renter. He was the first of many unimportant humans who would inhabit my upstairs.

The first renter was short-term, staying for one month, and when he left, the sister cleaned the upstairs, reset the advertising signs, and the interviews began once more. She, as manager, was allowed the task of interviewing and expected to make good decisions about the additional humans who would live in me. The others were busy with their individual obligations and jobs and trusted her to arrange it all. She did. There was an old ledger from her teaching days, and into this she wrote notes, kept financial information, listed the renters' personal claims, made suggestions for herself, and kept receipts for purchases. She was rigorous and thorough, methodical and detailed, treating her duties as if she were again preparing for her schoolroom teaching, and while she was the manager in charge, everything ran smoothly. That was not always the case in later years. When this family moved out and another moved in, the same rules and preparations and actions were not always maintained. Too bad. They could have learned from the ledger the sister left behind, but no one bothered to examine it. Eventually, decades later, it was found at the bottom of a kitchen drawer, forgotten and ignored, and once cleaning was accomplished, it was thrown out in the trash. The cinder alley told me that some of the pages had come loose and floated around him for a time, but in the snow and rain, they disintegrated. I always liked that human, the sister. She was a gentle sort. Still, sometimes during a quiet night, I pay attention to the babbling of the word-baby or the lowing of the ceiling cows or the scintilla of an assumed aroma from her flower garden, all produced from her words. If I could miss someone, it would be her.

Time, human time, continued. Renters came and went. Their words and sounds, their secrets and surprises, their human noises, both disgusting and amusing, continued to pack themselves into the floors and ceilings and walls, against the bricks and concrete and wood, pushing through and behind and into all the past sounds and words and stories, making me stronger and more resilient. But none were very memorable. So many of the conversations were repeats of past ones; the sounds, the words and stories, even, at time, the aromas jumbled together, causing me to warn them when they became extra clamorous that I would rip them from their spaces and send them out into the air to become obscured, obliterated, forgotten. Then they settled down. And more humans entered and lived and left and deposited their own sounds there, and I became bored.

Until sometime in the early part of the human twentieth century when a renter came and spent a longer time in me than others had. His name was…well, whatever it was, it doesn't matter. He stayed and was content to remain. He caused no problems and the sister and housemaid #2 who were the ones who dealt with him most often, were glad for such a quiet and seemingly gentle person, one who caused no trouble, to remain for the years he did. Frankly, I paid little attention to him for a long time until I began to notice his oddities, but I am not one to comment negatively about humans. They do that enough for themselves. Anyway, his story will be told. He was the first. The first who left something in me. The first whose secret is stashed away in a hiding place, exactly where he placed it in July of 1917, just before he went off to take part in another ridiculous human invention: war.

But his story begins before that. He met with the sister for an interview in 1915. She was impressed with the young man who had recently begun working in Chicago and was looking for a permanent place to stay. He signed a lease for one year, and then, signed another one. His story is first. His name? Fine. It was Robert Richardson.

6

Robert Richardson, 1915

Human emotions are trivial. They are so unsurprising that I play a game with myself: predicting the words which would be spoken and the feelings which would be hurt by them; anticipating the attitude, the disposition, the sentiments of one human or another. I am invariably correct and keep count of how many I have forecast correctly. It was, and still is, something to do. I, to use a human phrase I heard husband #2 use, *bat a thousand.* I watched as housemaid #2 began to do extra services for the new renter, Robert Richardson. Some Mondays she would sneak upstairs, leaving a clean towel for him and removing the used one, even though Thursday was the day for clean towels. Sometimes, because he did take breakfast in the morning, she would ensure he had extra oats in his dish, or place a pat of butter on top because it made the dull meal tastier. She would wipe his winter boots and clean the bottoms of them when during a rain or snowfall, he would leave them in the outer hallway. She mentioned to the sister that the boarder was "sweet-looking with a fine head of lovely hair", words which giggled their way to the corner of the kitchen, swaying and winking as they went. I was sure her flattering words were meant to find their way to his ears, meant to encourage him to look at her as more than a housemaid, meant to kindle a relationship of sorts. Once the cinder alley told me that housemaid #2 gathered with her friends, mentioning to them that the new boarder smiled at her meaningfully, thanked her profusely, watched her as she sauntered back to the kitchen after serving him breakfast. She was sure that at some point, a friendship and then a romance would be cultivated. She only had to wait.

I estimated that it would not happen. To be fair, I had the advantage. I knew what he was hiding, the secrets he was stashing away, the confidences kept to himself. I was able to hear him as he spoke softly to himself in his upstairs rented rooms, as he read aloud the notes and letters he kept banded up, as he examined, with a knowing smile on his face, the photographs he kept with those letters. And I watched as he and his friend visited together and walked down my front stairs to spend the evening with other friends and acquaintances, as they crossed the Boulevard and sat on one of the benches in the grassy area, talking and laughing and apparently glad to be together. His friend's name was James.

From their conversations I discovered Robert and James had been previously acquainted. During his initial interview with the sister, Robert did not tell her the absolute truth about his background. He told her he was originally from Indiana but had moved to Chicago after the death of his parents. He found a job in the downtown area and hoped to make a life in the city. He stated that there was no one except a distant cousin, James, whose address he could give as an emergency contact, if she needed one. The sister was understanding and reasonable, and eventually, when James came to visit Robert, he was introduced to the sister as that cousin. The two men would sometimes travel to the upstairs rooms to visit, and the family took this as a normal extension of a familial friendship. So did housekeeper #2. No one thought differently, and even when…wait, I can't get ahead of the story.

Some of what Robert said was in fact the truth, but, over time, I learned the partiality of his words. Yes, Robert was from Indiana, and when his mother died, he and his father had a major falling out. It was regarding James. During the argument, Robert's father called his nature *perverse, unnatural, and sinful.* Robert knew his father would not change his mind, so he left his Indiana home forever. I listened as Robert told James the words his father said. I watched, as bold and angry, those repeated words pushed their way to the top of the ceiling, demanding to have the best position, aggressively thrusting themselves into a space occupied by other words. I left them alone. So did the other words. There has never, in all these years, been a reconciliation. The strident words which were told to James remain there, lonely in their righteousness. Odious. Without chance of understanding or acceptance from his father, Robert left for Chicago. James, who had left before him, had written to him that it was easier to live in a city as large as Chicago, a city where, if they were careful, they might have a friendship, a life. So, Robert arrived, found work, and discovered my upstairs rooms.

I am genderless and sexless. Those concepts are strange to me, and even though I gendered the other houses around me, I only labeled them because I assumed readers would understand that, would be more comfortable with the usual categories. We are, in fact, all genderless. All sexless. Those human concepts don't matter to me, to us. From what I can tell, the emotions of *love* and *hate* and all the feelings in between are essential to humans. Strange creatures. Emotions often get in the way of accomplishing what is necessary. Robert and James were careful in their dealings. They assumed their masks of synergy, and remained, as housemaid #2 and the rest in the household knew them: cousins. No one ever found out otherwise. Except for me. And now you.

Human time passed, and in 1916, Robert began his second year in the rented rooms where his comings and goings and the *cousin's* visits were accepted. The polite inattention he gave to housemaid #2 weakened her hopes of a romance, and so, there were no more Monday clean towels or buttered morning oats for him. Not that he noticed anyway. Everyone seemed engrossed in their own inconsequential doings, remaining preoccupied with themselves. But by the fall of that year, the outside world was creeping into the thoughts and conversations of the humans, the neighbors who paused to speak to the family on my porch, the friends who sat around the dining table eating the stale cake baked by housemaid #2 and drinking the weak coffee the wife offered. New and strange words and names were abundant. *Re-election, Lusitania, Wilson, Germany, diplomatic relations* were some of the exotic words which entered the crack in the corner of the dining room ceiling, sent there by anxious and nervous voices. Circumstances and situations were stirring far outside my walls, but they skulked closer, incrementally pushing into my space, into the minds and out of the mouths of the friends, the neighbors, the family. And they were disturbing and distressing and disquieting as they crawled upward moving into empty places, taking up room next to ordinary words, making a foreign sort of racket. The most dismaying word, at first whispered, then spoken with more vigor, was pronounced. WAR!

Seriously. I heard the conversations, listened to husband #2 read aloud the newspaper articles, watched as anger and fear increased and not then, not afterwards, not even now, am I able to understand this human concept. Do you? I suspect not. But it took on a life, and through the end of 1916 and into the start of 1917, the thing moved from a ghostly specter to a fully realized creature, and soon there was no other discussion except for this one. In April, a man, Wilson, known as the President, asked a number of other men, known as Congress, to declare WAR on a country, known as Germany. At least that is what I heard again and again in the conversations at the dining table, on the Boulevard and my porch, in the cinder alley where the housemaids gathered. Then other words: *Selective Service, conscription, doughboy, Army,* made their way to the crack, and I realized these words brought with them a plethora of emotionally charged utterances I was unused to: *security, pride, uniform, marching, training, rifles,* and most feared by all the humans who spoke about this subject: *death.* As they were said, the words arranged themselves in two straight lines and instead of moving quickly to the ceiling crack where *Wilson* and *Germany* and the others were, they moved in formation around the space above the heads of the humans, weaving through each other, creating booming, threatening sounds as they grew larger. Quite unnerving! The humans could not see them, but I watched as they gave off sparks, smoke rippling out from their letters, fires starting intermittently, stopping before they burned up, creating an unhinged grouping. Had the humans seen this spectacle, they would have hidden under the table. Of this, I am certain. WAR was here.

James was conscripted into the army at the beginning of June, 1917. He visited Robert nightly until a week later, he was gone. Gone to be suited with an ill-fitting olive drab green uniform, feet shod in Pershing boots which were meant, but failed, to remain snugly dry in watery trenches, a Springfield rifle for which quick training was given. Gone to be inculcated with the precepts of the United States Army. Gone to *make the world safe for democracy.* Gone to be taught to kill.

Discussions about these things were held in the rented rooms before James left. Their words marched solemnly to the corners, following the instructions given (*Column Right, MARCH! Column Left, MARCH! Half-step, MARCH!*) by the largest word, the *Drill Sargent.* The two men laughed and mocked the training to come until the seriousness of the situation became evident. Laughter stopped. An awakening comprehension, a distinct apprehension took over. Consequential talks continued until James left. At the start of July, Robert Richardson awoke one Monday morning and did not go into work, but traveled to the Army Recruiting Station on 35th Street to join the United States Army, to do his patriotic duty, to help win the WAR.

He returned that afternoon, and I witnessed him in his rented rooms where he began to collect, group, and organize clothes and belongings. A few things were piled into one small valise, some into a larger suitcase, and the smallest grouping, the letters and notes and photographs he cherished, were placed on his bed, under his pillow. Later that evening, after he had informed the family he would be leaving in two days, after they wished him well, after housemaid #2 wiped her eyes as she stood in the kitchen listening to his announcement, he returned to his room to remove the items from beneath his pillow. He spent that night rereading the letters, grouping the notes as to their dates, smiling and crying at the contents. There were two photographs which he stared at for a long while. One was of James, looking out to the space in front of him, a somber, sedate expression on his face, his hands at his side, one foot a single step in front of the other, his body upright, rigid. The other photograph was of them both. They were laughing, arms thrust around each other's shoulders, a cap pushed back on James' head so that his hair was partially obscured. Robert held one, then the other photograph, a slight wetness in his eyes. He placed the photos on a table and walked around them. He held them to the lamp, examining closely. He pushed them to his chest, as if to mark their outlines into his heart. A great sigh rose up into the ceiling, gathering the other sighs which had been waiting there, becoming parent to them all. The great sigh held them together, making them one. Dawn was approaching. Robert had not been to bed. He wrapped the letters, the notes, the photographs together. He took one of his handkerchiefs and spread it across the bundle which he then wrapped in a massive amount of brown paper, tying it with soft string once, twice, three times, ensuring the package would remain closed and safe. Then he laid down on the bed, not bothering to remove his clothes. When the sun was high in the morning sky, he left his rooms to take care of whatever chores one takes care of before marching off to WAR.

That evening, the night before he was to report for duty, he sought out and spoke to husband #2.

"I have a favor to ask of you," he began, "When this war is over, I plan to return here and if the rooms are available, rent them once more. I am asking to leave a suitcase here because I was told not to bring personal items and clothing. I am just to appear in the clothes I'm wearing and bring only required personal items. The army will give me everything I need. Is it possible to place the suitcase somewhere safely out of the way so that when I return, I'll be able to retrieve it?"

Husband #2 nodded briskly. "Absolutely, my boy. Whatever you need to leave here will be safe. I promise that no one will touch it, and we'll look forward to your return. There is plenty of space in the basement. Get your things, and I will take you to the back steps."

Robert went to his rooms, returning with the larger suitcase. The husband took him to the outside staircase, used the key to open the door, and switched on a light for him. "There is plenty of space downstairs. Place the suitcase wherever you would like, and it will be safe. Turn out the lights and close this door behind you. I'll lock it later. Come and find me in the dining room. I believe I have a bottle of something so that we can toast your luck and healthy return. I'll see you shortly," and he left while Robert walked down the stairs.

The basement would eventually be made into a *garden apartment,* but other than some semi-framed walls and chalk marks showing where eventual rooms would be, it was a large, expansive space holding boxes and furniture from husband #2's old house. Robert looked about my lower level, looking for an out-of-the-way space to store the suitcase. He placed it against a far wall, tucked it into the framing, and stood still. He continued to study the space. When he found what he was searching for, he opened the suitcase, took something out, then closed it. He held the brown paper wrapped package containing the letter and notes and photographs I had seen him contemplate the previous night. I knew then that he wanted a hiding place for it. He wished it safe. He could not take it with him to WAR, could not take a chance that it would get lost or seen by anyone. He wanted it kept secure for him, for his return. He walked over to the space beneath the staircase coming down from the outside. He was tall and could not stand upright beneath it, but underneath the stairs, the space called the spandrel, were some boards which created shelf-like areas. He reached back to the highest one to examine it, to see how far back it went, and satisfied, placed the brown paper wrapped package into it. He pushed it as far back as possible, and, after checking again and then again, he seemed content. It would be hidden from view. No one would find it, and when he returned, he would be able to retrieve it. He glanced once more at the suitcase containing his extra clothes, a newer pair of shoes, his Sunday hat, some socks, and winter things, walked up the stairs, turned out the light and closed the basement door. He went inside the house to the dining room where husband #2 waited with an almost full bottle and two glasses which were filled halfway with an amber liquid. During the following hours, their accelerating laughter and merry words rose tipsily from their lips to the ceiling and walls, swaying and swerving into each other, bumping and weaving and coming to rest at lopsided angles. The two men toasted to the country, to winning the war, to success as a soldier, and to Robert's rapid and reliable return.

    The year of WAR dragged on. Husband #2 read from the newspapers, and I heard nothing except articles about battles and news about what was happening in France and other countries which held no importance or interest for me, and I grew bored of the entire business. When neighbors stopped by, when family came over, the talk was the same. Only one time, in the fall of 1917, did the family receive a brief letter from Robert thanking them for being kind to him, explaining that he had been trained as a soldier at last and he was headed overseas. He was not sure where he was being sent, but was anxious for the WAR to be done so that he could come back to the rooms and see them all again. Husband #2 read the letter aloud twice, and the words he pronounced presented themselves as distressed and jumpy. As the words were read, they traveled in an unsettled way, seeming to glance around, twitching at unfamiliar sounds, cowering together when they reached what they thought was a shielded area. When the letter was laid on the sideboard in the dining room, housemaid #2 took it and reread it to herself many times as she stood in the kitchen, tears filling her eyes. She had never totally given up her hopes of a relationship with Robert, and the tears and quiet sobs clung to the side of the pantry where they remain in sad disarray. Silly girl. She would have been better off saving that energy for the cleaning of my kitchen walls.

That was the only letter they ever received from him. Sometimes the wife would look through the mail and then say to the sister or housemaid #2, "Nothing from Robert. I hope he is safe and this WAR will be ended soon. I'm sure he will come back here as soon as possible," and she would give a slight shrug of the shoulder and go back to her work. Although the upstairs rooms had been cleaned and the signs replaced in the windows, there were no takers for the rooms. I thought the wife was more concerned about the rent they were missing than Robert's return. Only once were the rooms rented for a short lease, one month, by an older man who was "just passing through" as he said, but when he left, they remained empty for a long time. Few men were available to rent them due to their being busy with the WAR.

The year of 1917 ended and 1918 began. Winter snow was tracked onto my floors; spring mud was brought into the kitchen on the housemaid's shoes; summer heat caused the icebox ice to melt on the floor; fall leaves filled my backyard. I noted the seasons by the messiness they brought to me. Then, another letter arrived

Not a letter like the usual mail, but a telegram delivered by one of the boys who rode a bicycle and came directly to the houses, the sort of job the son used to think about having before he left. It was the type of letter no one really wanted. At least that is what the sister said when she answered the door. She gave the delivery boy a nickel, and he was grateful. Then he tipped his hat and said, "I'm sorry, Ma'am," because he knew what he was handing her. The sister answered the door because housemaid #2 was at the grocery store. Had she been home to answer the door, the delivery boy would not have gotten that nickel. The sister shut the door and stood with the thin envelope in her hand.

"Who was that?" called the wife from the dining room where she was working at measuring and cutting some material to make new aprons. When the sister did not answer her after a second inquiry, the wife came out to investigate. She saw the sister standing and holding the telegram, and it seemed to me that they both knew what it was before opening it.

"He must have given this as his home address," said the sister, and she handed the unopened envelope to the wife who was reluctant to take it.

"I suppose." answered the wife. "Should I open it or wait for my husband to get home?"

The sister shrugged. "We know what it says, and there is no sense in not opening it. Just read it."

The wife handed it back. "No, you are better at reading things. Go on," and they acted as if the thin sheet was a disease-riddled monster which neither wanted to handle.

The sister took the envelope and opened it. It said:

November 8, 1918

The Secretary of War desires to express his deepest regret that your son,

Private Robert Richardson

died of wounds received in battle on November 6, 1918.

Letter to follow.

As the words were read, they created a sound similar to a bugle softly playing, and together in a black cloud-like mass, moved to the nearest wall, just under one of the roses created by the Irish plasterer and his son. There they remain. The two women stood still. The sister wiped her eyes.

"Poor lad. The army must think we are his family. So sad that he has none to receive this sad news. What should we do?"

The wife shook her head. "I don't know. Perhaps my husband will have an idea, and as soon as he gets home tonight, we'll let him read it and decide what to do about it. You know, I believe the housemaid was sweet on him. She may take it hard. Should we say something to her?"

"Yes, she should know. After all, they are close in age, and..."

There was a noise at the kitchen door and they heard housemaid #2 come in. She placed some things on the counter, took off her coat and hat, and entered the parlor. When she saw the sister and wife standing together, saw the telegram held in the sister's hands, saw the expressions on their faces, she placed her hand to her mouth to keep in the scream-sob which quickly escaped and raced to the ceiling to huddle next to the black cloud-like mass. "No!" she choked out. That afternoon, it was the wife and the sister who made her some tea and sat her in the dining room chair and handed her their handkerchiefs as she cried.

On November 11, 1918, the WAR official ended.

Holiday celebrations in 1918 were subdued. Housemaid #2 asked for some time to visit her family, and everyone thought that was a splendid idea. After all, she had moped around the house, barely completing her duties, inattentive to the cooking which suffered from additional inattention, and sometimes sat at the small kitchen table, dishes piled up at the sink, the stove needing fuel, the icebox door left open, and tiny silent tears fell from her eyes into whatever it was she was half-heartedly stirring. She was told to take some time and return after the new year, so she did. The wife and the sister divided up her duties which kept them both extra busy. In January of the new year, an older man came to stay for a short lease of three months, and the wife seemed happier. Money was always welcome. When housemaid #2 did return, she seemed better. Only once or twice a week did the tears fall into her mixing bowl, and by the spring of that year, everything was back to normal. Thankfully. Human emotions are exhausting. And annoying.

According to human time, it was a Saturday in May when a deep cleaning of my interior and exterior was taking place, and I was feeling a satisfaction due to the needed attention. Gleaming windows were opened to allow fresh breezes to billow through my sparkling rooms, the steps and porch were scrubbed, the walkways were given a brushing. My bricks shone in the sunlight, and, had I been able to, I would have known pride. As the cleaning ended, I was conversing with the Boulevard. We did not interact often, but I was feeling neighborly, and it was an exceptional day. The grass and flowers had begun their prominent blooming, and the sight was creating gladness. It was then, just as the Boulevard commented upon the Mayness of it all, that I saw him come around the corner. He looked tired, and there was a definite limp as he walked unhurriedly down the street to my gleaming steps. He stopped in front of me, looked up to the windows in the rented rooms, and an anticipatory smile appeared on his face. It took him a while to come up my stairs due to the fact he had to drag one foot up each step, but he maintained the smile as he knocked at my door.

The sister was in the front parlor wiping the wooden furniture with a polish and a rag. She was first to get to the door, and stopped in complete surprise when she saw him.

"Why, Mr. James! Hello. I am surprised to see you. How are you?"

James answered, "I am better. I was wounded in the war and spent a long time in the hospital, but I am as good as I am going to be. I was released just a few days ago and have traveled to Chicago to see Robert. We lost touch during the war, but he said he would be coming back here and we agreed to meet as soon as we could. I see the upstairs windows are open, so he must be home. May I go up and see him?"

The sister was shocked. She hesitated before answering, then said, "Please come in and have a seat here. I will go and find my brother and be right back. There is some news."

He remained standing inside the small hallway. The sister returned with her brother, and the news which James did not know and was not expecting, was told to him. It is a good thing husband #2 was present, because when the words *Robert* and *dead* were uttered, James fell against the doorjamb and was caught in the arms of the larger man. He was partially carried to the dining room table where he collapsed into a chair, put his head down into his arms, and sobbed.

Well, more crying. Great. Not helpful to me. And it was such a lovely day. I was feeling so good about my cleanliness, my sparkling windows, the grass and flowers, and then this happened. Then, more sobbing when the wife appeared and housemaid #2 came in from hanging clothes in the backyard. They cried as water and tea and, for some reason, a plate of cookies were brought into the dining room and placed on the table. Handkerchiefs were passed around, and once everyone gained control of their emotions (I can't even describe the words and sobs and sounds which were all tangled up in the air, bumping into each other, excusing themselves loudly, and moving in such muddle and messiness that all the other words and sounds peeked out from their places in the ceiling and walls and floors to view the commotion.), a sort of orderliness settled. Housemaid #2 went to her room and brought out papers to hand to James. These included the solitary letter written by Robert, the sorrowful telegram received by the family, and the solemn letter they had received from the War Department extolling the bravery of Robert and his valiant effort to remain alive after being wounded. Robert was shot during something called the Meuse-Argonne Offensive in France, died of a serious infection, and was buried in France in a cemetery with other brave soldiers. Honestly, I was unsure how brave he was because it seems that all soldiers are called *brave*, and I suppose it took some sort of courage to wear those ugly drab olive-green uniforms and carry that heavy rifle. Well, mea culpa. Chalk my spitefulness up to having to deal with humans and their emotions

James read through the paperwork. Then he wiped his eyes, and sipped the tea. Small talk continued. He asked if he could keep the papers, and everyone was silent, waiting for the housemaid to decide an answer. She looked at the man who, had things turned out differently, might have also been her cousin one day, and said, "Of course. The papers should stay with a family member. I'll find a folder so that you can keep them together," and she left. The faux cousin did not correct the assumption about their kinship.

Husband #2 looked at James and spoke. "Before Robert left, he asked to keep a suitcase here. He planned on returning and had no other place to store his extra clothes. It's downstairs, and if you would like it, I'll get it for you. There may be some remembrances of him in it."

James seemed unable to speak, so he just nodded his head and took another silent sip of his tea. There was total quiet in the room, and everyone at the dining table could hear husband #2 open the back door, walk down the stairs, and then back up, footsteps echoing on the wood. He came to the dining room holding the suitcase which had been stored awaiting Robert's return. He placed it next to James saying, "There it is. I hope you're able to find things in it to remind you of your cousin." Those words left husband #2's lips and smirked their way to the ceiling in a cunning manner. He knew what was in the suitcase. He had opened it and examined the items, thinking to find something of value in it. There were only clothes and a few books and some inconsequential personal items. The only thing husband #2 could find to keep were two brand new pairs of Durham socks. He wore them to church on the Sundays he and the wife attended Mass.

James looked down at the suitcase and then up at the man who sat down next to him. He took a last sip of tea, and then sat back looking around at everyone.

"Thank you. I'm happy to have this, and I appreciate your past kindnesses to Robert and now, to me. I must go. I need to make some plans and check the train schedule. I'm going back to my home in Indiana. My sister said I could stay with her and her family until I completely heal and decide what to do," and James stood up and reached down for the suitcase which was lighter now that two pairs of socks were gone.

Housemaid #2 handed the envelope containing Robert's information to James who smiled his thanks. Everyone walked him to my front door and hands were shaken before he left. Husband #2 and the wife stood on my porch and waved to the man limping to 35th Street where a bus would take him to his temporary hotel room. He held the suitcase protectively, and before he disappeared around the corner, turned and waved once more. Then he was gone.

The wife looked at her second husband and said, "I am glad you thought to give him that suitcase. I hope he finds comfort in it."

"So do I," he replied, "so do I."

Perhaps additional comfort could have been offered if James had been given the brown-wrapped package containing his letters and notes and photographs. Perhaps he wondered if Robert kept them, or took them to war with him, or destroyed them, because if discovered, they would be considered reprehensible to some. Perhaps James had his own brown-wrapped package of letters and photographs hidden safely away, a balm for his future. Who knows? What I do know is that the first secret, the hidden package containing the truth about the men, the one Robert thrust far back into the shelving under the basement stairs remains there. Remains sequestered. Remains private. Remains a discreet, obscure witness to one of those annoying and difficult to understand human emotions: love.

6½

A Follow-Up

So, there it is. The first story. The first secret. The first hidden item. Now you know who, what, when, where, why, and how. All the elements of a news story, except it's just a mediocre tale about a human whose actions were not important. Just the standard script. But the words and emotions left behind by all the humans helped to make me stronger. Settled into my walls and bricks and ceilings and floors and joists and nails and on and on; all of them creating my potency. Remember, I was young when these first secrets occurred. I was naïve and anxious. I did not know how important these stories would be to my soundness, to my hardiness, to my stability. But I learned.

James? I have no idea what happened to him. Did he stay in Chicago? Return to Indiana? Die in a fire or a fight? Who knows? Not important, and if you think he is or his story is, then you are missing my point. It is not humans themselves who are important…but I won't continue. I will assume you understand. Anyway, no one ever heard about James after he turned that corner, suitcase in hand, traveling to his third-rate hotel where he probably, sobbingly, pondered his future. I hope his numerous tears and overwrought emotions helped strengthen the dirty four walls of the room he slept in that night. Enough about him. As far as the original family's story, they will continue into the next narrative because they are still part of it.

And, before that begins, I did promise some of the other parts of the neighborhood they will get some space in this book, my autobiography. The Boulevard is the first to have a go at it. Read his words next. Or don't. I don't care. You can always skip to the chapter after his: the one about the Hodgkins family. Their story is astounding. Astoundingly awful. What a group of humans!

Go on. Read something.

7

The Boulevard

I am older than Red. I have memories going back many years: to the Natives: the Ojibwe, the Odawa, the Potawatomi people who traversed my path, the dirt path, from the south to the north, and eventually to the west. Later groups: the Miami, the Fox, the Kickapoo came, traveling, stopping to hunt, to explore. They traded and went northward to the waterways, first to the north branch of the river and then east, into the larger lake. The tribes beat down the grasses, cut the branches, made their way down this path, down me. When others came: white settlers, mixed-race people, Europeans, they built small wooden structures and then larger ones close to the river. When the town expanded, my path became the western border of the place called *Shikaakwa*, Chicago, and Western Avenue, my name, came into being

I have undergone many changes. Eventually, my wooded and leafy dirt paths gave way to hard-packed dirt and wooden plank roads where human traffic, horses, wagons and carriages of all sorts walked, dragged, rode, trekked. The wood planks dug into the dirt making me a thoroughfare, and I became aware of the movements, the sounds, the extended travel along me. Not all of it was pleasant. Imagine the horse droppings from the riders and wagons, the pig and cattle excrement as those creatures were moved from farm to farm, the vomiting of the many men who over-imbibed at the inns and taverns along the way. I apologize for the images, but I have put up with many unpleasant occurrences in my time. Bricks were placed to brace up the wooden planks which split as the mud and rain continued to smother the earliest path, and as civilization continued its so-called progress, gas lines and electric service lines were laid down, covered by asphalt and concrete, and through the centuries I changed. Walkways, sidewalks, curbing, became common, and I was often in need of repair as winter weather caused cracks and splits, and large sores called *potholes* appeared, needing to be repaired later in the springs and summers. Changes happened slowly at first and then rapidly until something occurred: I became a twin.

Twin. That word is appropriate and will allow humans to understand. I split, becoming both Western Avenue, the original me, and Western Boulevard, the part who tells this story now. In the early part of the twentieth century, plans for creating a series of medians containing trees and grassy areas for humans to enjoy the outdoors in what was becoming a crowded and congested city, were made. Along nineteen established thoroughfares throughout the city, boulevards and park areas came into existence. At the start of the human twentieth century, I came to be. I am a tad more than three miles long, while the entire avenue is about twenty-eight miles from far south to far north. Longest street in the city, so I hear. My length and age and experience over the years allowed me to remember the many conversations, proceedings, incidents, diversions in the median where the open space, trees, and flower beds encouraged humans to wander, to play, to converse, to sit on the wooden benches placed systematically throughout the median, and to breathe what was once fresh air. Not now of course, during this modern era of massive traffic, of smoky trucks, noisy buses, innumerable automobiles and a spattering of motorcycles, but in the past, when these items were scarce and expensive to own, and humans walked from one area to another. Over one hundred years ago I could hear the voices and conversations easily. The words and emotions hung in the cleaner and clearer air before they sank into the grass and dirt of the median, under the cement and asphalt, the bricks, the split wooden planks, into the hardened dirt and then the softened mud and deep, deep into the earth where there is plenty of space to store the centuries of words in a multitude of languages. My ability to know, to understand, was how I came to realize the secrets of those men, the ones Red wrote about: Robert and James.

I noticed them as they emerged from Red together for the first time. They stood outside on his porch, glanced around, and one of them pointed to the median. The other nodded. They crossed me and walked down the area, stopping periodically to examine where they were, shifting occasionally to allow young boys and girls to run past as they chased a ball or each other, and when they came to an unoccupied bench, they sat down and were silent for a time. One of them (James, I think) sighed and the conversation went like this:

"Was it that bad?"

"It was. He called me a sinner, a vile creature. He said he was ashamed of me, and I needed to leave his house. He said he was glad my mother was dead because this would have killed her anyway. I was told to get out by the end of that week."

James looked away and there was a stillness before he spoke. "You never told him that your mother knew, did you?"

"No. What was the use? I didn't want him to think badly of her too. I knew what he would say and was sure about what he would do. I didn't wait until the end of that week. I packed that night and took my suitcase and the small valise. Early the next morning, I left as soon as it was light. He was still in bed. I walked miles to the next town where there was a train to the city. I left a note for him, but have never heard anything. When I moved here, I didn't bother sending the new address. It's over."

There was another silence, Robert looked at James and said, "Anyway, you're my family now. We are all we have."

There was more talk along the same lines. They were hoping to eventually find a small apartment together. James said there were neighborhoods in Chicago where they would be accepted, although they would continue to introduce themselves as *cousins*. That was best, he said. That was safest. Their words floated up and intermingled before they drifted down, entering the space beneath the bench, curling under the grass and dirt and the lone dandelion which lingered. For months, the two men would come to this wooden bench and sit and share their thoughts, plan a life together, laugh about things, wonder when they would have saved enough from their meager earnings to find that perfect place they could make their home, living as cousins. Then, that thing humans call *war* occurred. Their last conversation was a sad one.

They were seated on the same bench, heads bowed, words spoken softly. James told his friend he was leaving in the morning. He was being sent to a place in another state to be trained as a soldier. He would keep in touch as much as possible, and when the fighting was done, when the conflict was over, when the battles were completed and the bodies buried, he would return, and they would do what they had dreamed of doing for years. They would find a place together. They would start a new life, a happy life, and whatever the hardships, they would endure them as a couple. Those quietly spoken words were taller than others. They rose with hope, with a purposefulness not observed before. They lifted high into the air, waited, and then together, as a band, plunged into the ground, rustling the grass, moving the bits of dirt with the robustness of their joy and fervor.

Robert looked up, nodding and smiling. "We'll meet here at the house. If I do join up, when I return, I'll come here. You'll be able to find me; I'm sure the family will take me in after the war. Then we won't put off our plans any longer. Let's shake on it," and he held out his hand.

They shook hands, holding on longer, squeezing tighter than was necessary, but that handshake contained an encyclopedia of words and emotions. They finally let go.

You know their ending. Red said it was told in his story, so I won't repeat it here. Funny thing about that bench they occupied. Over the decades, many of the benches became so used, so weathered, that they split. They became unserviceable. The city replaced some benches with new ones made of a material that was meant to last longer than the original wood, and others were simply removed and thrown away. But that bench, the one the men sat on as they planned their lives, still remains. Oh, it's beaten up; some of the wood is splintered and cracked, but it remains, waiting for their return. But there was none. And there never will be. Their words and emotions remain deep in the earth, under the weathered bench. Periodically, if I listen carefully and the surrounding noise is minimal, I can still hear the muted joy, the muffled fervor. There is a discreet hope which lifts up, poking the hardened soil, forever caught, unable to break through.

I am done. I thank Red for this opportunity. He was specific that I could only have a brief space to tell *my* story and to say what I know of *theirs*. He wants me to stop now. So, I will.

8

Hodgkins Family, 1921

I have not hidden my disdain for the human race. A generally boring lot. And yet, I admit the beneficial relationship which there is between us. I even admit to having a soft spot for a few humans. But mostly, the mundane emotions, the substandard actions and thoughts, the unpolished simple ways of the majority of them are obvious. Oh, don't take offense. After all, if you are reading this, there must certainly be something in you to admire. By someone.

For years, I was indifferent to the humans who trickled in and out of my upstairs rooms. For a time after that WAR, there wasn't a great demand for the rooms, and the family, especially husband #2, was nervous about the lack of rental income. There were angry words between husband #2 and the sister. He accused her of being "too picky" and added, "This isn't your classroom. Stop turning renters away for stupid reasons." Those words marched in righteousness to the ceiling, turning and stamping what might be called their feet before slamming an imaginary door. Husband #2 got what he wanted. The sister accepted the next group who came to inquire about the rooms. And that is how the Hodgkins family entered the picture. *Disdain* does not seem a strong enough word for how I felt about them. And, eventually, how the family did too.

I noticed the man, Sam Hodgkins, walking down the boulevard examining houses. I thought he was admiring them, but then realized he was looking for a quick way in, an unlocked door, an open basement window. I learned of his past, of their past because, I always do. No human secrets are hidden from me. His first secret: he was a criminal. Not a very successful one because he and his family needed to be continually on the move, but he was sly and crafty enough to stay ahead of any real trouble. The first time he came to me, he stopped and looked at the sister's sign in the front window advertising the rooms for rent. Not many humans had ventured onto the porch and knocked at my front door to inquire about the rooms, but the following day, Sam returned with his wife, Nelly. That is how he introduced her to the sister when she interviewed them. His second secret: not his wife, not married. Third: actually, distant cousins, brought up together and raised to be scheming and conniving humans. The interview with the sister was brief. She was inspired to rent to them and determined to prove to her brother that she could still manage the upstairs, so her questioning and investigating was not as thorough as her previous interviews had been. A mistake on her part.

"So, Mr. Hodgkins, it is just you and your wife who will rent the rooms, correct?"

"Actually, my dear," and his words were cagy and calculating as they squirmed into the air, looking around with a smugness I have rarely seen in human discourse, "our son, we call him *Junior*, will be with us. He is currently at school. Such a wise young man! So smart and reliable. A genius, a real scholar!"

His wife, speaking with the same smugness, nodded and smiled and repeated, "Such a scholar, so proud!"

Fourth secret: not a scholar. In fact, and I learned this after they moved in, they weren't quite sure where he was that day. Or most days. Yes, their son, Junior, had been sent to school, but his actual whereabouts were often unknown. Fifth secret: not their son. That story was reviewed in whispers as they spoke nightly, arguing about whether or not to tell him. He was a baby when a friend of theirs (co-conspirator most likely) died of a large amount of tainted alcohol. Nelly felt bad about leaving the baby to starve, and talked Sam into taking him, justifying that action by saying their appearance as a family would lend a needed air of respectability. So, he was adopted into their group, brought up in their ways, inculcated with their seamy outlook on life. Secret six: Junior was unaware of his origins. He thought himself their son and was ignorant of these secrets. And when he did discover them, well…you will find out. Continue to read.

The first month's rent was paid and a three-month lease signed. The sheet listing the rules was read and agreed to. An old mattress was moved from the basement to the first upstairs room, settled in the alcove under the window: a makeshift bedroom for Junior. With this done, the Hodgkins family became the newest renters. Husband #2 was satisfied. The sister was relieved. Accommodations, responsibilities, and commitments were accepted by both groups. Everyone was satisfied. But, as always, being cognizant about what was transpiring in my upper rooms, I waited for the catastrophic to happen. It did.

The first month's rent was paid, and the Hodgkins family had opted for partial board, so they ate breakfast each morning. Quite a lot of breakfast, actually, and Junior was the biggest eater of all. He could swallow two bowls of oatmeal, four slices of bread, and whenever additional food was available, consumed as much as he was allowed. After all, explained his father to housekeeper #2, he is a growing boy, and his schoolwork should not suffer due to hunger. I watched as the growing boy shoved an extra piece of food into his pocket to be consumed later, and housekeeper #2 saw it also. She didn't stop him or say anything. I heard her tell one of the neighboring housekeepers that although Junior was taking more than his share, she kept quiet. "I remember being hungry as a kid. There never seemed to be enough food for all of us," she reported. "I am pretty sure there are days he doesn't get any more to eat." That part was true. His parents provided a morning meal, and he was expected to provide additional food for himself. Sam told Junior that this was his personal responsibility, that he was only *helping to make you tough*, to *make you a man*. And Junior, forced from a young age to do this, became adept at pilfering whatever food he could from various sources. He was adept because, secret seven: Junior, from the time he could stand upright, was instructed in the censurable art of thievery.

Lessons were given during evenings in the upstairs rooms. Sam and Nelly would take turns playing the part of Upright Citizen, and Junior was expected to take something from them: a wallet, a watch, some jewelry, something of importance, something which could be traded or sold or pawned. To ensure success, a small bell was attached to the Upright Citizen's person, and if heard, Junior's attempt was considered a failure, and his ears were boxed. Or he was slapped or pushed, or, if the bell rang too often, shoved onto the floor and kicked. Junior made few mistakes. He became almost as excellent a pick-pocket as his faux father, Sam, who spent his days working the streets of Chicago, practicing the art of which he was a master. If the nightly lesson was considered a total success, Junior was rewarded with a bit of change to buy himself a special treat the following day. He looked forward to those few perfect lessons because, unbeknownst to Sam and Nelly, he had a plan. And his plan involved needing a certain amount of cash.

A comment is needed about the words of the Hodgkins group. In all the years human words have escaped into my walls and floors and ceilings and bricks, I have never worried about their repercussions to my own steadiness and support. The angry words, the sad ones, even the mild oaths all joined together, linking, unifying, integrating with each other or with like clusters, assembling, structuring, codifying and in their unity, creating security for me. As they should. Except for those words coming from the mouths of Sam and Nelly. They were weak. I would watch as the words climbed lazily to the ceiling or a wall, slinking and sliding their way, losing parts of themselves before they got very far. Slivers of letters sloughed away, drifted to the floor, atrophying and collapsing and disappearing from sight. The sections of the words which managed to enter into a wall or ceiling were transparent and partial, and I am convinced they did no actual work at their arrival. They leaned their fragmented selves against each other and tried to cozy up to the words there, the ones who were doing their jobs, who were harmonious and companiable. In other words, (pun intended), the false, dishonest, weak words came from the false, dishonest, weak mouths and corrupted minds of the Hodgkins couple. Junior's words sometimes had the same effect, but only when he was with his fake parents. When he was alone, speaking to himself, planning his future, the words were different. I listened to his constant quiet patter as he lay on the mattress by the alcove, thinking out loud about his future, planning his eventual escape, his words filled with juvenile hope, shifting unsteadily but constant to the walls as he murmured to himself each night.

Junior did not like the people he assumed were his parents. They showed no affection to him, wanted no bonding with him, offered no guidance to him with the exception of the thieving lessons. Junior was not even told his actual name or age. In fact, no one remembered those items. I listened to Sam and Nelly reminiscing about Junior's entrance into the family, and if I could have helped Junior escape sooner than he did, I would have. Don't think this is an example of that emotion called *human compassion*. I am not human. I have no compassion. I disliked Junior. But I disliked Sam and Nelly more. Humans who resided in me should be grateful, and their speech should support me. The Hodgkins' words did not. Sam and Nelly spoke about the times, years ago, when they took Junior from his dead mother before he was two years old. They called him *Junior* and gauged his age from that instant, so while he did not know either his birthdate or actual age, Junior was almost two years older than he was told. Nelly would often declare to a shop owner that her baby boy was celebrating his birthday and oh, she wished she could afford to give him an…apple, piece of cake, cookie, bite of salami… whatever she thought would be offered by a kindly owner. Sometimes it was, and Junior was taught to thank the owner profusely, turn to Nelly and say, "Look, Mama, look at what the nice man/woman gave to me!" This happened at least a half dozen times each year, so Junior never knew if it was actually his birthday or not. It worked until Junior, at the ripe age of almost twelve (actually almost fourteen) had grown a few chin hairs, developed a lower voice, grown an inch taller than his mother, and Nelly realized her *baby* was no longer going to receive free treats. Instead, she directed Junior to snatch something from a nearby counter while she engaged the shop owner in a discussion about the ripeness of the cheese or the staleness of the pastries. None of which she would purchase anyway. And Junior's parental monitoring would continue.

Back to his plan. Junior had attended many schools as the group moved from one place to another. At times, it was necessary for them to find an empty stall or a small niche or a corner of a barn to spend the night or a few days. Money was a continual problem, and when they could afford to, small rooms were rented, although they never stayed in one place for any length of time. The money ran out, or they were discovered for what they were, or the police chased after them, running them out of one town into the neighboring one. When they were settled again, Junior was placed into the local school as a sort of safe keeping while Sam and Nelly went about their daily business: pick-pocketing, stealing, swiping, shoplifting, burgling, looting, sometimes falling in with like-minded individuals and forming a brief bond. Junior knew no other life. But because of his experiences at the many towns and schools with which he became acquainted, he knew there was another way to live. He wanted that way. He also knew it would involve having a stash of cash and being a certain age. *Fifty dollars* and *thirteen years* were the magical numbers. I listened to him review his plans nightly, the quiet words rising rose-colored, in youthful animation and solidarity. He would lay on the old mattress, and by the light of the moon seeping through the window under which he lay, he would whisper the plan, a self-encouragement, a prompting, a pressure, an inducement to himself as he did two things. First, he would take out his stash and count and recount it. Some paper bills and coins were his. They were hidden in a brown envelope he had taken from some teacher's desk, carefully folded in two and held tight by a rubber band he had found. Junior was careful to rarely spend the treat money he earned for his perfect thieving lessons. He knew that any money he had obtained needed to be handed over to Sam. Once or twice, he did not, and he had a specific memory of the punishment doled out to him when coins were found in his pocket. He became more careful and less greedy. A coin was hidden before the rest were offered to Sam, before his pockets and person were examined. He knew that his few personal items and his mattress were checked because he would come home finding his things in disarray. A hiding place Sam and Nelly knew nothing about: a loose floorboard in the corner, away from his mattress, away from prying eyes, away from the few items he owned, held the banded envelope filled with some bills and coins. At latest count Junior had one precious ten-dollar bill, a five, four singles, three nickels and two pennies: $19.17. A little over thirty dollars to go.

His age was an issue. Not knowing exactly how old he was or when he would attain the magical age of thirteen was frustrating. A few times he asked Nelly exactly when he would celebrate the next birthday and exactly how old he would become. She was always vague about it, answering, "What difference does it make? You're here, ain't you? I suppose you're ten or eleven now. Big for your age, but, that's a plus. Now, go on outside to the streets, and see what you can bring in which is useful." And Junior would go, finding or stealing a few pennies, keeping one and bringing the other two to Sam. His offering, a tribute for his protection, for the avoidance of physical chastening.

And what was Junior's escape plan? There were few schoolbooks which kept his attention, but one seemed to provide a solution. Not the McGuffey readers with their character building and moral lessons which were plain silly. I listened to Junior sneer at their stories. A dog is hurt and then cured. A turtle turned on its back is uprighted. A boy kindly frees a caged bird. A child finds a coin and returns it to the poor woman who dropped it. This last story had Junior in such stitches of laughter that Sam demanded he stop the hooting sounds which scrambled awkwardly into the corner of the ceiling, shaking and heaving with emotion. Arithmetic books were tolerated, but once the basics were learned, they were useless. Who cares if Mrs. Jones spent eighty cents and gave the clerk a dollar and received a certain amount of change? The clerk should have charged eighty-five cents and kept the extra nickel. But the geography book was a treasure. So much of a treasure that Junior snatched one from a school and kept it. It was full of maps of the United States. Maps of places to travel, to wander, to escape. So secondly, after the stash was counted and recounted, after the envelope was rehidden under the floor, after the maps were reexamined, his fingers would travel across the states, heading west, looking for the place where fifty dollars would take him. Then, Junior put the geography treasure aside and fell asleep. I suspect he dreamed of the day he would have the exact amount needed to pay for a train ticket to the West. He would even spend some on a new hat, if one could not be stolen. Having reached that magical age of thirteen, he would board the train, stare out the window at the passing city, glad to be away from those people who claimed him, delighted to start a new life, excited to at last, be released from his impoundment. He would drop the name *Junior,* would baptize himself anew, and as he fell asleep, he would mouth the various names he might choose. *John, William, Charles, George, Richard,* would float quietly and happily from his soon silent lips. I would see them gently lift up in the moonlight, find a place in a convenient space, nestling against *Edward, Thomas, Donald, Harold*. Possibilities.

He would stare at the bathroom mirror, examining his face, running his finger over the baby hairs that grew upon his upper lip. He would measure himself against the wall, looking at the height change from the last time he stood there, remembering that he could easily look down upon the top of Nelly's head, noticing that it was just a couple of inches until he could meet Sam's eyes straight on. I wondered if he compared himself with the other fifth graders, gauging height and chin hairs, seeing that he was as tall as the boys in the eighth-grade class, looking from beneath his lashes at the eighth-grade girls who wondered about the new tall fifth grader. One night, he came from the bathroom where he had noticed his pants were too short, his facial hair was darkening, his measurement against the wall had increased, and he closed his room door and stood for a time thinking. He spoke softly to himself, cursing Sam and Nelly, feeling larger and stronger and muttering: *I have to be thirteen. Maybe fourteen. I need to work on getting more money. I must get out of here.* His anger, his resolution came from the discovery of some pennies he had hidden in his back pocket. Sam found them. Junior had been in the bathroom spitting out the blood which had accumulated in his mouth. Punishment. He decided to increase his stash quickly.

School attendance became spotty. Junior left the house each morning, walking towards the schoolyard, but I saw him reach the end of my street and turn the opposite way. Apparently, he walked the neighborhood, taking note of which houses were empty during the day, which ones had a loose window or open door, which ones had careless owners who had left yard tools leaning against a garage or fence. I know this because he had drawn a map of the neighborhood in the blank page of his pilfered geography book, whispering to himself about the possibilities which he checked with his pencil. On the other side of the page, he listed addresses of pawn shops and second-hand stores. Places Sam did not patronize. Shops which would give a few pennies for a new rake or a man's clean shirt or a birthday toy a careless child had forgotten to bring inside. Just a few pennies because the young man had offered these items with a sad story. *My mother is sick and needs some medicine, and I must sell my little sis's toys. My father died, and I am selling his best shirt so we can pay our rent. My grandfather gave us this almost new rake, but we no longer need it since we must sell our house.* Stories and tales told with sad eyes and a downturned mouth. I know because I heard Junior practicing his spiel during the night, words hurrying towards the ceiling, quiet and stealthy, glancing around, worried about being stopped. They sometimes clashed with the snoring sounds made by Sam and Nelly, which squeezed under the door between the rooms, wheezing and snuffling up the walls. And little by little Junior's stash grew. $20.14. $20.76. $21.03.

It was important to keep the money hidden from the adults. The next month's rent was due and Sam and Nelly did not have it. Too much money had been spent at the corner tavern, and since saving and budgeting and planning for the future were not among the abilities possessed by either of them, the tenth of the month passed, and the sister did not receive the required rent money. The next day went by, and the next, and the next, and the sister waited at the front door when Nelly entered on the fourteenth day of the month. She was stopped before climbing the staircase to the second floor.

"Rent was due four days ago," said the sister, "I need to have it now." She used her best teacher voice, and the words which were strong and strident and stern surrounded Nelly, waiting.

Nelly smiled a large phony smile and answered in a weaseling manner, "Of course. I am so sorry. My husband should be home soon and will have the money for you. Thank you for the reminder. My, don't you look nice today? Have you done something new with your hair?"

The sister did not answer. She was reminded of nonsense compliments from students who also offered excuses for missing assignments. She crossed her arms, looked gravely at Nelly, and after a full thirty seconds, stepped aside so she could go up the stairs. When Nelly got to her room, she opened the window and waited until Sam was in sight. She waved him away, and the sister never got to confront Sam that night. It was midnight before he stumbled back, crawling up the steps. It was a matter of hide-and-seek after that.

Day nineteen. By this time, the sister was sure no rent was forthcoming, so she had to go to her brother with the sad news. The Hodgkins family had not yet attempted to come into the house, so husband #2 locked and bolted the doors and waited in the front parlor for the inevitable ring of the doorbell. When it jangled, he went to the door, opened it, and stood behind his sister who had assured him she could handle it, but he should stay close. Sam and Nelly stood on the porch.

"Where is the rent?"

Sam nodded and reached into his pocket pulling out some money. They had worked hard at their craft and had been able to filch a partial rent. He held out the bills and some coins, and in an attempt at being pleasant and agreeable said, "It has been a difficult month. Here is about half the rent, and we will have the rest of it in a few days. Thank you for your understanding. You must know how hard it is. We have been attempting to help out some dear friends who are in dire straits, and at the risk of our own welfare and that of our son, we gave them the rent money. You know what the good book says about helping our neighbors and seeing to those in need."

None of them actually knew what the good book said, but assumed it was something important. The sister looked back at her brother and a small shrug from him let her know that something was better than nothing. Husband #2 reached around and unlocked the door allowing the thoughtful couple in, but before they went to their rooms, he said, "Until the rest of the rent is paid, there will be no breakfast for any of you in the morning. Is that clear?" Those words, rigid and rough and resolute, marched to the wall and stayed there, glowering down at Sam and Nelly who nodded their understanding and scooted up the stairs.

Sam, Nelly, and Junior, went without breakfast for the rest of the month. The following month came. Day ten. No rent was forthcoming. There was no waiting for day nineteen and on day eleven, the doors were locked, and as housekeeper #2 looked on from the kitchen, the sister, the wife, husband #2, and a friend of his who was on the Chicago police force all waited in the front parlor for the Hodgkins to appear. They were to be evicted. The lease which they had signed stated this would happen upon non-payment, and the family realized that this group of untrustworthy renters would need to be removed. It wasn't just because of non-payment. Items were missing from the house. The wife could not find new cutting shears she had recently purchased. Housemaid #2 was constantly missing food: four pears instead of six, a large chuck of cheese was gone, a small slice of ham disappeared. Husband #2 looked all over for a carpenter's square and some hand tools he needed. When late one night, housemaid #2 heard a squeaking on the back stairs, the staircase which ran from the upstairs rooms to the kitchen area, the mystery of the missing items was solved. A decision was made. A plan was in place. And on day eleven, in early evening when Nelly returned home, she was surprised at the door being locked. She peeked in and the sister unlocked the door so she could enter. Nelly's mouth opened at the sight of a uniformed police officer standing in front of her. She did not know he was not there in an official capacity, but as a friendly gesture to husband #2. The sister closed and locked the front door. No escape.

Husband #2 spoke first this time. "You are behind in the rent one and a half months now. According to the lease, you and your family are being evicted. My wife and I will accompany you to the rooms and watch you pack just your belongings. When your husband and son are here, you all must leave unless you and your husband have all the rent required plus next month's rent too," and those words left the husband's lips but remained just above his head, linking their letters together, shifting from side to side, ready for a fight. Anxious for one.

Nelly was frightened, and there was nothing for her to say. The police officer glared at her, and she shifted her gaze to the floor and was silent. The wife started up the stairs followed by Nelly who was followed by husband #2. They walked up to the rooms where Nelly retrieved the old suitcase and the small bag and began to pack their meager items. She was watched carefully, and when a drawer was opened and the wife's shiny new cutting shears were spied, she cried out, "Ah ha! You are thieves besides freeloaders! I knew it!" and those words were spewed out in all capital letters, dark and thick, swarming around Nelly's head, refusing to lift up to the ceiling. I thought that I would need to intervene, the words were so outraged. Nelly quickly finished the packing, then the three of them went to Junior's room where his few clothes, some papers, and his geography book were shoved into the small bag.

While the packing and shouting was going on upstairs, Junior came to the door and was told he must remain downstairs while his mother packed their things. There was a panic in his being. He was going to push past the sister and housekeeper #2, but the police officer stopped him.

"Stay right there, boy. You can't go upstairs. Your Ma is packing your things."

Utter dismay, total hysteria were the emotions oozing out of Junior's being. His face turned red. His hands clenched and unclenched. His arms shook. "I have to go upstairs. I HAVE TO!" and his shouting filled the room. "I HAVE to get some of my things!"

The police officer shook his head and stood on the bottom stair. "Your Ma is getting everything. She'll bring it down. Stay here, or you will regret it." He meant it. He had dealt with these wild kids before and knew how to handle them. He knew what to do. He would not hesitate.

There was yelling and pleading going on, words making no sense coming out of the mouth of Junior. He didn't know what to do. He was aware of what the police could do. Would do. He had seen it before.

Had even once, just a few weeks ago, been on the receiving end of such actions, and this time there was no alleyway for him to run down, to escape. Worst of all, he could not let Nelly know what he wanted. What he needed. What was hidden under the floorboard in the corner of his room, in a brown envelope, protected by a rubber band. How would he get it? And if he did, Sam would take it. Would possibly have to pay what was owed. And then, the punishment which would be doled out to him would be even worse than what the police would do. It was there: the money he had found and earned and stolen and traded and pawned. The means of his escape. The method by which he would purchase the train ticket and travel West. Traveling across the states on the rails as quickly as his fingers walked across the maps in the back of his stolen school book. He could do nothing. It was upstairs. Hidden. His hope; his aspiration; his dream. His $32.45.

The trio from upstairs came down to the parlor. Husband #2 had not helped Nelly carry down the suitcase or the bag. He would be no gentleman to this woman, this thief who was charged with bringing down her own items. Behind Nelly was the wife who carried the rediscovered cutting shears in her hands. When they reached the front parlor, the police officer took his place on the bottom stairs just in case the wild kid attempted to go up to the rooms. He looked at Nelly.

"Do you have your things?"

"Yes," she responded.

Junior jostled Nelly and asked, "Did you get all my stuff?"

She looked at him, shoved the small bag into his arms, pushed him away and said, "It's all there. Everything."

Junior knew it wasn't, but he opened the bag and searched through it, hoping to find a brown envelope. Knowing he would not. Hoping he would not. He spoke again to the police officer, "I need to go upstairs. I need to check again. There might be something she forgot."

Nelly looked at him, her eyes suspicious. "What did I forget? Is there something else I don't know that you have?'

Junior was struck silent. No use. He could not admit there was a hidden envelope with cash in the room. He was thwarted. He was frustrated. He was defeated. He shook his head, and said "No", and that word dragged itself to the side wall and stuck there. It had no ability, no strength, no capacity to go farther. It slowly dissolved, falling to the floor where it would be carried outside on the bottoms of shoes within a day. A sad ending.

Husband #2 made a decision. "Do you know when your husband will be home?" and he waited for Nelly's answer.

She shrugged her shoulders and shook her head.

"Well, you are finished waiting in here. We will go out to the porch and wait for him. You are no longer welcome in this house."

The entire group, led by husband #2 and the wife, still holding the shears, then Nelly carrying the suitcase and Junior clutching his bag, after which the sister, the police officer, and housekeeper #2 walked out the opened front door. They stood on the porch glancing at the sunset which was a brilliant orange and pink, although none of them remarked on its loveliness. Small talk forbidden. It was not long until Sam was seen turning the corner, walking down the boulevard, hat pulled low on his head, hands in his pocket, lips pursed and a whistling sound slowly fading as he saw the group waiting for him. He did not walk up the walkway. He did not climb the front steps. He did not ask what was going on. It was obvious to him what had happened, and he stood just in front of the bit of grass and was silent.

"Do you have the money owed to these people?" and those words rang out from the police officer's lips, landing with outrage just above Sam's ears.

"No, but…"

"Don't bother with your lying excuses," yelled husband #2, "You and your family are evicted. Your things are packed and I suggest you leave this area before you are arrested," and he pointed down the stairs as Nelly and Junior hurried to join Sam who waited at the edge of the walkway.

Nothing else was said. The three of them hurried away. The group on the porch stood and watched them leave before reentering the house where husband #2 and the police officer checked and rechecked each and every window and door, ensuring they were locked and bolted. The door locks would be changed in the morning. The sister and housekeeper #2 went upstairs to check around the rooms, making sure nothing was missing. They discussed what would need to be cleaned the following day. The wife, after placing her newly found shears in her dresser's top drawer, went to the kitchen for the coffee and cake they would share as they reviewed the evening's events. An hour later, when the police officer left (after shaking the hand of husband #2 who palmed a couple dollars into the waiting hand of Chicago's finest), the women cleaned up, readying themselves for bed. Husband #2 rechecked the locked doors, bolted windows, turned out the lights, and joined his wife in their bedroom. An eventful night. Before going to bed, the sister found some clean paper and placed it on the dining room table. Tomorrow she would rewrite the sign for the window advertising rooms to let.

They did not know what I knew. They were unaware of the drama that was taking place in my back yard, under the stairs to the back entrance way, during the dark and gloomy midnight hour. The Hodgkins group had returned. I did not know immediately what had happened after they slunk away from the house and my observation, but later I was told. The Boulevard saw them turn the corner onto thirty-fifth street. The corner drugstore watched them as they hid between the buildings. The small diner listened as they huddled in her back table, eating the cheapest blue-plate special and drinking plenty of water as they decided what to do, where to go. None of them had eaten much over the past few days, and some food was necessary. A next meal was uncertain. Where they would spend that night was unknown. It was Junior who came up with the plan. I was informed the conversation went something like this:

> *Sam:*   *How much cash do we have? I have three dollars.*
> *Nelly:*   *I have about two dollars.*
> *Junior:* *Forty-eight cents.*
> *Sam:*   *Great. And these meals will cost $1.20. Hey! More bread here! Either of you have a bright idea for later?*
> *Junior:* *Let's go back when they are in bed. We can sleep under the stairs. There's an old blanket there.*
> *Nelly:*   *That will work for tonight. Maybe we can get back in tomorrow.*
> *Junior:* *I'll check the basement windows.*
> *Sam:*   *Fine. Well, Junior, you are almost smart enough to be my real son. Almost, anyway,*
> *Junior:* *WHAT DO YOU MEAN?*
> *Nelly:*   *Stop, Sam. Not tonight.*
> *Junior:* *WHAT'S GOING ON?*
> *Sam:*   *Nothing. Lower your voice, you dolt. Come on, Let's get going.*

There was probably more to it, but those are the bare bones of the conversation as I was told about it. The diner said that after they ate more bread and drank more water, they paid the bill (no tip) and left.

The waitress was sore and yelled at them "Don't bother coming back."
They left and wandered the streets until all the stores were closed, the
lights were out, and they circled around to the cinder alley in back of the
house and creeped into my yard. The cinder alley let me know that they
were continually arguing. Junior wanted to know what Sam meant by
saying he wasn't their real son; Sam was annoyed by his questions and
angered by the night's events; and Nelly was trying to keep them quiet
and maintain a peace. *Ugly people*, claimed the cinder alley, and frankly,
he should know *ugly*.

They all stood in my yard, determining whether it was safe for
the night, but having no place to go, they made a space for themselves
under the stairs, spreading the old blanket Junior found under their
bodies. As Sam and Nelly made themselves comfortable, Junior traveled
around the house, trying all the basement windows, sneaking up to
the outside doors, examining any way he might get into the upstairs
rooms. He wanted his stash. Everything was tightly locked, and finally,
in despair, he joined the others under the stairs. They were a miserable
crew, and spoke in noiseless whispers. Junior demanded to know about
the comments Sam made. He would not let this go, asking repeatedly,
his words becoming more aggravated, more annoyed, more exasperated.
Sam looked at Nelly. They muttered in muted tones to each other.

"We were going to tell him anyway. Might as well do it now. No
sense in hiding the facts." Sam turned to Junior and for perhaps one of
the first times ever, told him the truth. "I ain't your Pa. Nelly ain't your
Ma. You ain't related to us. Your real Ma died from bad hooch, and we
saved you from dying with her. Called you *Junior*. Raised you. Might as
well know now. You are old enough; actually, about two years older than
you think you are. That's the way it is, boy. Now you know. Shut up so
we can get some sleep. We need to leave at early light," and Sam settled
himself back, parental duty done. Words streamed in sordidness towards
the bottom of the wooden stairs where they attached themselves, glaring
down in unseemliness at the counterfeit son.

Junior had more questions, but none received answers. He was
ignored. He was shocked. He was angry. He was relieved. There was
nothing keeping him here now. He just needed his stash, but there was
no chance of getting it. He sat back against my bricks and watched as the
people to whom he no longer owed allegiance fell asleep. He sat for an
hour, and I could tell he was creating a plan. A new one. A revised one.
As Sam began to snore softly, he adjusted himself for comfort, and as he
moved to his back, his jacket fell open. Junior glanced at him, squinted

at the open jacket, eyes widening as he observed the concealed wallet which Sam had not mentioned but had kept hidden. Junior, a slight smile on his face, did the thing for which his phony father, his instructor of the underhanded arts, would take pride. The action which would mark Junior as his true son. If not through blood, then through deed. Junior picked the pocket of Sam. No bell rang. No movement was felt. There was not even a slight repositioning or a minor shifting of material as the wallet was perfectly and exactly lifted from the inside pocket of the sleeping Sam. Junior sat back, and in the faint light of the moon, pulled out of the wallet three five-dollar bills, four singles, and two quarters. $19.50. It was not the $32.45 which was hidden in a brown envelope under a floorboard in the room upstairs, but it was enough. Enough to get a ticket on a train and travel West. Enough to buy some cheap meals when hunger pains started to bother. Enough to leave these sleeping, stupid people who stole his birthdate and name and life. It would do.

Junior looked at the wallet. It was poorly made and there was nothing else in it. He considered replacing the bills and keeping the whole thing. He had never had a wallet. As he stood there, another smile appeared. He nodded his head. He didn't need the wallet, but he needed to leave a message for Sam and Nelly. He settled the bills and quarters deep into his pants pocket and set the emptied wallet next to the sleeping Sam. He left it open so it would be obvious it was empty. Junior almost laughed out loud, but placed his hand over his mouth so the noise would not escape. The thought of Sam waking up at first light, seeing the empty wallet, knowing who took his hidden cash, delighted him. He looked around for his bag which held his few items and picked it up. Glancing at the adults sleeping there, he made a gesture with his fingers, one I knew was meant as a nastiness, and he began to walk towards the alley. He stopped and returned. He removed his worn-out cap from his head and placed it next to the open and empty wallet. His signature. Then he reached behind Sam and with the adroitness and nimbleness taught to him, lifted the adult's hat and placed it on his own head. A good fit. One glance back at the open, empty wallet and his own tattered cap, and he left. He walked quickly down the cinder pathway to the end of the alley and let out a sound which I could not interpret. He turned right and disappeared. Gone.

There is no need to review what happened when Sam and Nelly awoke. You can guess their outrage, their indignation, their lividness It was clear they had been duped, and by their own son! The one they had saved, had raised, had trained! They packed up. Sam flung Junior's signature cap into the yard of the yellow-brick house where it fell into the tall weeds which grew along the fence. He stuffed his empty wallet into his pocket, hastily folded the old blanket which they took with them, and left before being discovered by housekeeper #2 whose morning movements were becoming audible. Upon reaching the end of the cinder alley, they turned left. I suppose to look for another neighborhood, perhaps a nearby town, maybe hoping to run into that boy they had saved, had raised, had kept alive all these ten or twelve years. Sam knew what he would do to him, and as he cursed the boy, narrating the actions he would take once they met up, those words which left his lips trailed behind him, following as quickly as they could, pushing and shoving each other, growing larger and meaner. The fuming words followed Sam, and were in turn, followed by Nelly who moaned as she attempted to keep pace with her husband/cousin's furious, blistering tempo. The Hodgkins group: Sam, Nelly, and Junior, or whatever he decided to rename himself, was gone. Their words: the nasty ones, the untruthful ones, the angry ones, the deceitful, humbugging, duplicitous, rankling, aggressive words remain. They may be vile. They may be vulgar. They may be malicious. But they continue as a strengthening agent for my walls, my wood, my stairs, my red and righteous bricks.

8½

Again: Additional Changes

$32.45. Junior's hidden treasure. Still there. Still under the corner floorboard in a brown envelope wrapped up in a rubber band. Even the sweeping and polishing and moving of furniture along that area never pushed up the board. Never caused any of the humans to glance down, to see a loose corner, to lift it up, to find the treasure. That small bit of money would not count for much today, but decades ago, it would have been quite a find. Worth about ten times what it is now. One of the changes.

After the Hodgkins family left, a few short-term renters came, but none wanted the rooms for a long period. The humans residing in me were getting older. The wife was having trouble with her eyesight, so her seamstress business was faltering and the ease of buying ready-made clothes was making her work obsolete. At least that is what she said, and those words left her lips and tearfully attached themselves to each other as they tried to find a restful place near the wood baseboards. They did not have enough strength to get to the ceiling or the walls. They mirrored the wife's physical ailments. She had more issues than poor eyesight. She began to cough and wheeze and was eventually diagnosed with some kind of wasting disease. After doctors recommended it, husband #2 took the wife to an institute west of the city, one which would look after her and cure her. Didn't happen. The wife took to her bed, coughed until she could not make any more sounds, and died one afternoon just before husband #2 showed up for his weekly visit. Her death led to additional changes.

The sister and her brother spent many evenings discussing what to do with me. Rent money was meant to form a nest egg and complete the downstairs apartment, but neither goal was met. A small nest egg was available, but my downstairs remained as it was decades ago: dusty and dirty and filled with unwanted furniture. The sister, having kept in touch with friends from the small town in Indiana where she had taught and lived with her husband, discovered that her old farmhouse was, once again, up for sale.

"We could live there together, and you would like the quiet and ease of a small town. The surrounding farmland has been sold and new houses have been built on it. The town is expanding. We could live there cheaper than here, in Chicago, and the money would go farther. What do you think?"

"Maybe," answered the brother, "I'll retire soon. Let me consider it and do some figuring and talk to a few people. I wonder what we could get for this place?"

Plenty, as it turned out. Especially since husband #2 never had to use his own money to obtain me decades ago, and the mortgage had been paid. Anyway, they decided to move to the old farmhouse, found a buyer for me, a new human group moved in, and additional changes took place. Some of those were advantageous for me. And now, it is necessary to differentiate between the groups of humans who lived in me, and I refuse to bother with their names. So unimportant. This group will be, Group Two (G2), and the next will be Group Three (G3). You catch on, don't you? I will assume you are able to understand. Over the years, I have learned never to underestimate the stupidity of humans. Don't take offense. You know that to be true.

So, G2 paid the price and moved in, but before they did, alterations were made. My rooms were given a needed repainting. After decades, the original paint had darkened, and in places, was peeling. The downstairs bathroom was redecorated and updated to match the style of the late 1920's. The ancient kitchen appliances were replaced with newer ones. The old stove gave way to a new gas stove, and the old icebox was replaced with a new-fangled refrigerator, so that ice didn't have to be hauled in two or three times a week. The kitchen floor was covered with something called *linoleum* which I thought rather ugly. Additional cabinets were installed along my one wall, and I will admit I was quite proud of the updated look. Except for the linoleum. A new sort of washing machine which contained an attached wringer for the wet clothes was hooked up next to the large wash tubs in the basement, and the back stairs which had turned rickety and weak were torn down and replaced with a newer, sturdier set. But the biggest change was the garage. That building butted up against the cinder alley and encroached into my yard, something I was at first upset about, but later…well, keep reading. The garage housed G2's new car, a Ford Model-T. The G2 husband didn't want to park the thing on the street where the Chicago weather would damage it. I heard him announce this to the G2 wife a number of times when she questioned the cost of the garage. For the years they lived in me, G2's arguments were mostly about the time and care and money spent on the upkeep of that Model-T and the subsequent cars bought by the husband.

The G2 group: husband, wife, two daughters in high school, were a typical family and one which did not, for a time, need to worry about money. I heard their conversations about things called the *Stock Market, Investments, Capital Gains, Industry*, all things about which I was uninterested. Apparently the G2 husband had *made a killing* with these things, so he bragged to his friends. He worked in the downtown area at some large building made of a material called *terra cotta*, with reinforced concrete. Frankly, I was unimpressed, being of fine red brick, but I heard the husband describe the new building numerous times on the newest appliance in the house: a telephone. Once all the updates were finished and the family moved in, the south end of the front parlor was organized as an office for the husband. A desk, a rolling chair, a smaller bookcase, were arranged there, and the telephone was installed and set on the desk. Sometimes the husband would work from what he called "my home office", and this new device received much use. It was unnecessary for the wife to work and earn money, so she did not. She spent her days shopping, talking to friends, meeting for lunches, chatting with her Ladies' Club and such. A useless life. She grew friendly to housekeeper #2 who was kept on to work for the family. She and the G2 wife were often in the kitchen, sitting at the new table there, drinking coffee and discussing the antics and behaviors of neighbors. The two daughters were quiet, and I appreciated that. The older was in the last year of high school, while the younger was in the second year. They were close and content to share a bedroom even though they were offered the upstairs rooms as their own. "Eew, no!" they said, "It's creepy up there!" and I watched those words scurry up to a corner and shake until they melted into a small ceiling crack. That left the upstairs empty. There was no need to obtain additional money as rent. At least not at that time. Later, it would become a necessity.

I settled down and watched and listened to their mundane conversations, the silly giggles of the girls, the wife's complaints about the cost of the Model-T, the husband's plans to revise the basement apartment at some point, and I was, to be frank, a bit bored. I was grateful that the constant chatter helped to support my walls and bricks and wooden structures, but worried about the upstairs which received no extra support because it was empty. Eventually that also changed. An older relative on the wife's side needed a place to live, and she began to talk about allowing the man to live in the rooms. In late 1927, after numerous discussions, the G2 husband agreed to this, and just as the Chicago winter was beginning, the rooms upstairs were once again in use. Uncle Henry moved in.

9

Michael Henry Davis
aka Uncle Henry
aka Professor, 1928

There is a species of sharks in Greenland whose life expectancy is somewhere between 250 to 500 years. On the other hand, the aquatic Mayfly lives for one day. Hummingbirds live from 3-5 years; mice live about one year; a bee might live up to two months. Various fish and tortoises might remain alive for up to 200 years, and the oldest human was a French woman who lived to be 122 years. These are facts I have gathered through my decades of listening to school reports from the children living in me, or science articles and news reports which were read aloud. Most humans have a lifespan somewhere between the Mayfly and the French woman, but there is always an end. I know of some of the ends, have heard about others, and have reached a verdict. Humans would like the lifespan of the Greenland shark, or at least an Orange Roughy (about 100 years), but periodically, a human wants, for one reason or another, to cut it short. Allow me to introduce Michael Henry Davis.

Michael Henry Davis. *Uncle Henry* to his family. *Professor* to his friends. Dubious designations. Michael Henry Davis was not really an uncle to the G2 wife, but she had called him that for years. When the G2 husband asked for clarification, it was given like this:

"Well," and the G2 wife squinted her mouth a bit and narrowed her eyes to help her think, "he might be my stepmother's brother, but…no that's not right. Perhaps he is my dead mother's cousin once removed and…no, wait, I remember my father saying something about his mother's brother or maybe it was stepbrother. Or uncle. I'm just not sure. Uncle Henry has been called that for years, and when I was young, he was at most family holidays, and once he went on a family vacation with my sisters and me. And I know he was at our wedding, wasn't he? Yes, he was seated with my other uncle, my real uncle, you know, the one with the pipe and glass eye. Anyway, he is a perfectly lovely man, and he needs a space, and will be no trouble. He has to leave the apartment he has been in for years because…not sure why, but I know he has friends who will visit to keep him occupied, and he is a poet, you know. Won't it be wonderful to have such an artist in our house? I can probably ask him to speak to my Ladies' Club. Perhaps he will read some of the poetry he has written. I think some was even published. You know, he taught for many years at some marvelous and exclusive boys' institute…where was that now? But then that is why his friends call him *Professor*, although I have always known him as *Uncle Henry*. While we don't need the money, and I know he has only a small pension, he is willing to part with some of it. In fact, he insists upon paying some rent for the rooms, and I can't talk him out of it, and we will simply put that money aside for a special vacation or something. And that is the explanation about our relationship."

Those words jostled out from the wife's mouth, knocking and bumping into each other in a confused manner. Many of the letters were horribly mixed up, and as they rose to the ceiling, they spread out, colliding and smashing and ploughing through each other until the words were so mixed they weren't words any more. Just a mash of letters looking around at each other in astonishment. The G2 wife generally spoke exactly like this, and, frankly, I never became used to the dishevelment. The G2 husband just sighed and said, "Fine." Uncle Henry moved in the following month, just in time for the Thanksgiving feast.

I am so astute at deciphering the stories and histories told, I was able to settle on a partial truth about the man who moved into my upper rooms. Michael Henry Davis was born during the country's Civil War, grew up in an insignificant town, received a trifling education at some mediocre small college somewhere in the Midwest, and began to teach, poorly, I assume, at a non-descript boys' academy nearby. He taught there for years, earning enough to support only himself but never a wife. Once he published some little ditty he had written in a local newspaper, and called himself a *poet* after that. I admit to not knowing too much about this human art of *poetry*, but I have heard Uncle Henry recite some of what he has written in the green ledger he keeps, and…again…wait and find out for yourself. Suffice it to say, Uncle Henry, the Professor, was a poet in the same way Junior was a scholar. As to his actual relationship with the G2 wife and her family, that was never sorted out.

I will come right to the point about this third hidden secret. It was the green ledger containing the so-called poetry of Uncle Henry. It slipped behind the built-in bookcase in the first upstairs room. I think it was a mistake, but before Uncle Henry's…umm…departure, it may have been done on purpose by him. I am unsure about this. The ledger itself was worn and frayed at the edges. It was obvious he had it for years, moving around with it from place to place, and it was a valued treasure to him. He wrote in it with small cramped letters, starting at the top of the page, continuing down to the very bottom, ignoring the margins at both places, and used the front and back of the sheets. The book was about three-quarters filled when he moved in, and at the end of his stay, there were about three or so pages left blank after the last poem he wrote. Sometimes he would read through the book from front to back in his soft lilting voice (never a commanding one, and I doubt he ever had full control of a classroom of young males), stopping periodically to wipe a tear from his eyes because he was so touched by his own efforts. Had I any eyes, I may have joined him in tears, although mine would not have been from appreciation. Here…I have pulled a couple lines from the wall to allow you to admire the kind of prosy (probably not *poetry*) of which he was so proud:

> *And oh, oft, in wonder at the cloudy skies well above*
> *Do I sit and picture thee, oh, joy, my love.*
> *With hair of golden curls around thy, oh, so lovely face,*
> *adorning a worthy, happy smile so filled with peaceful grace.*
>
> *My heart is oh, so filled with glee and joy*
> *That, oh, I am honored to be your wordless boy.*

I do not understand to what he is referring. His mother? Why is he *wordless*? And *honored* to be so? Perhaps this is about another woman? Is this a love poem? Why is the word *oh* used so often? And so poorly? There's much more to come; brace yourself. Many of the (AHEM!) poems have the theme of love, mixed with nature, and are confusing at best. There were times he wrote the start of a poem, maybe two or four lines, and never finished the thing. He would walk around saying those lines again and again, but could never complete them. For example, this was one repeated much too often:

> *Little tiny tweeting bird*
> *Sitting on the branch*
> *Singing out a noted word*
> *And with a rapid glance…*

What? With a rapid *glance*…what? Did the bird see a cat? Was the glance from the bird at all? Maybe the poet glances at something? At times he would change the word *rapid* to *frightened*, or *grateful* or, and this one I never understood, *thunderous*. What *tiny bird* has a *thunderous glance*? Or even a *grateful* one? Can birds have those feelings? I doubt it. The words in this particular bit were spoken so often by him that they rose up to the corner, joining additional, previously spoken words who pushed together, allowing them some room at first, but eventually, after a dozen of them were there, the older words began to shove the newly spoken words and lines to the back. It was a jumble, a shamble. There were many instances like this. Uncle Henry loved his own words. He loved his voice too.

And to be fair, his voice was quite melodious. At least it seemed so upon his arrival. Soon afterwards, there was a raspiness to it which I noticed. Perhaps the G2 family did not. Or they may have just ignored it. Ignored its cause. Even then, when he was speaking what I considered nonsense, even when the raspiness occurred, his voice was never coarse or unpleasant, and I could appreciate the sound even though I came to deplore the actual words. Uncle Henry looked the part of a professor. At least that is what housekeeper #2 claimed. He was tall and thin, becoming thinner as time progressed. He had a head of brownish-colored hair which was both thinning and graying at the sides and longish at the back and always looking as though it needed a decent combing. Not that it was ever dirty, just a bit messed. This was probably due to his habit of pushing it back as he wrote or read. He wore his spectacles (that is what he called his eyeglasses) perched lower on his nose and was forever pushing them up with his thumb, although he generally missed, smudging the glass portion. About every fifteen minutes, he would take them off and clean them on the scarf which he usually threw around his neck, no matter the weather. He became progressively chilled. He rotated the wearing of the three suits he owned which were in style several decades ago, but always dressed as if he intended to give a schoolroom lecture. He was a neat man, although at times he wore two different colored socks, and while he seemed to prefer a long tie over a bow tie, unless he was going out, he simply draped the scarf (he owned two, both some shade of gray) around his neck and was prepared for his day. If he left the house, Uncle Henry would take his homburg hat with him. He did have an old straw boater which he wore, but only when he gardened.

The garden. What a project it became! By late winter, Uncle Henry had eased into the family. He was friendly with the daughters who thought him a silly but harmless old man, and he gave sufficient praise to the husband who smiled and nodded and said little to him. Uncle Henry praised housekeeper #2's average cooking and baking, and so entertained the wife's Ladies' Club that he became a regular attendee when meetings were held in my dining room. And one night after a perfectly average cut of beef had been served with oversalted potatoes and undercooked carrots, the family sat back to partake of the coffee and dry poundcake served for dessert, and Uncle Henry spoke up. He cleared his throat several times first.

"I have noted that there is a rather large and grassless space by the garage. It gets much of the daily sun, and if you would like me to, I could do some planting of flowers there. In my youth, I used to garden alongside my mother, and when I lived in a small house during my teaching years, I grew many flowers and even some vegetables. It was a hobby of mine. Would you mind if I took up that hobby again in that area? I believe it would be delightful to see an array of blooms in the back."

The husband looked up and shrugged. "I have no objection to that. Suit yourself," and he went back to chewing mightily on the dry poundcake.

The wife answered, "What a wonderful idea! I would be happy to see flowers back there. I, myself, have no green thumb, but my grandmother had that lovely garden in the back of her large yard. Oh, Uncle Henry, do you remember it? I believe you spent some time there when I was young. What sorts of flowers will you plant? Girls, perhaps you would like to help Uncle Henry with his project. Do you think you would? I am sure the Ladies' Club would appreciate fresh flowers on the dining room table for our summer meeting which is in late June, and I suppose I should begin to plan for that, and what a wonderful idea. My grandmother…"

I cannot continue reporting her nonsense. She went on like this for quite a time, the words flowing from her lips, lifting and mixing and bumping and becoming annoyed with each other. The end result of this conversation was that Uncle Henry began to garden in the yard, wearing some bibbed overalls over his clothes and the straw boater on his head. I have no idea where the overalls came from, nor do I know when the gardening boots he wore appeared, but he was decked out in this outfit and spent much of that spring outside in the small muddy patch which, to give him his due, he turned into a pleasing flowerbed, one which surrounded the garage on two sides. I admit, it vastly improved the looks of that shingled garage, and then, I didn't so much mind the loss of the yard. The daughters did no gardening.

If there was a downside to the whole thing, it was in the form of many nature poems written in the green ledger. For example:

Patch of green with colors so bright
Red and orange and yellow and white.
Lifting up your face to the sun,
Gracing the yard for everyone.
A garden, a garden,
A note of delight,
A tumble of beauty
Oh, oh, oh, what a sight!

Uncle Henry loved reciting this little ditty, and when he sat at the June Ladies' Club meeting, wearing a red and blue striped bowtie which peeked out from under his ever-present scarf, the women, who I assume were completely uneducated, clapped loud and long after the recitation which they insisted Uncle Henry repeat. The words rose to the corner of the room, dressed in various pastel shades before melting into a mess of color together. I listened and was sure that the second recitation contained at least four *ohs* on that last line. Painful.

Besides gardening and poetry writing, Uncle Henry owned a passion for playing Dominoes. When friends visited, he pulled out the tiles for a game. The winner would be treated to coffee and a piece of pie at a local diner by the loser, and with the high stakes agreed to, the game would commence. The friend who came weekly was a man named Daniel Jenkins, or, as Uncle Henry called him, *Jenkins*. Jenkins called him *Professor*, and while I don't know when their friendship started, I believe it was at a school where they both taught. Jenkins would come on Wednesdays about one o'clock in the afternoon, and they would talk and play the game, and a couple hours later would travel to the diner on thirty-fifth street for their coffee and pie. Uncle Henry would return right before the evening meal was served, but on Wednesdays, he never joined the G2 family at the dining table due to his claimed fullness from the coffee and pie. He never ate much at breakfast except for some tea and a slice of dry toast, always skipped lunch, ate a minimal dinner, and the family assumed his growing thinness was due to his picky eating habits. Not quite.

Around the first of each month, Uncle Henry would get up early and ready himself for a trip. Before leaving, he would remind housekeeper #2 he would not return until later, and would not want supper. His scarf wrapped about his neck, his homburg on his head, his umbrella on his arm, he walked to the corner streetcar stop and waited patiently. He was gone all day, and upon his return, he wearily climbed the stairs, opened the bedroom door, and plopped into a chair, not removing coat or hat. He whispered to himself, "How long? How much more?" and those words had difficulty edging up the walls into the ceiling. The front letters pulled up the rear ones, helping them, encouraging them to continue despite their sluggishness. Eventually, he stood, removed his hat and scarf, and reached into his coat pocket to remove a small brown vial. There were some tiny words printed on it, but I did not hear what the vial contained because the Professor never read it aloud. Instead, he quickly put the vial into a drawer in the dresser next to others just like it. The vial was small and could not contain much of anything, but he kept them all there, pushed into the corner, covered with a handkerchief.

You can probably guess where this is headed. Uncle Henry would not have the lifespan of the Orange Roughy. His thinness and poor appetite, his tiredness and the eventual wheezing cough he endured were symptoms of an issue he had been aware of for some time before coming to live with the G2 family. The only other person he briefed about his menacing illness and looming fate was Jenkins, and even then, he downplayed the problem. Jenkins noticed the thinness and haggardness and cough of the Professor, whereas the G2 family, busy with the upcoming graduation of the older daughter, occupied with plans for completing my basement apartment, engaged in spending the money the G2 husband was making, paid no attention to Uncle Henry, his occasional disappearances, his reticence at the dinner table, his increasingly skeletal appearance. Jenkins noted the discomfort and disorder of his friend, and on Wednesdays as the two men worked at Dominoes, they spoke quietly, Uncle Henry answering the inquiries from Jenkins in a vague and tempered manner.

"Yes, I have," and Uncle Henry answered without looking at Jenkins, keeping his eyes on the dotted blocks in front of him, pretending to concentrate, furrowing his brow to give that impression. "I have seen someone. No, there is not much to be done. Yes, I am at ease. No, I will be fine," and he glanced at Jenkins while pushing up his spectacles with his thumb and gave a slight smile. "Domino! There, I guess you will be treating me this time!" The subject was dropped, and the words spoken slid up into a space in the wall, trying to look normal, attempting to hide their lankiness and angularity, hoping to appear the same as the other words they skittered next to.

Through the months, Uncle Henry continued his daily activities. Although he did not sleep much at night, but sat in a chair, arms wrapped around his perceptively narrow, meagre body, he made daily early morning visits to his garden. Even on dreary days, he would walk out before the G2 family was awake, check the flowers he planted, pull out invasive weeds, encourage the lowered blooming heads to take in the rain or the dew or the sun, smile as he did so, took pleasure in the sprouts, the shoots, the seedlings. He would whisper softly to the plants, "You are looking splendid! Yes, I can see your growth from just yesterday. Good job over there! Wonderful colors. You appear elegant and noble! So proud of you!" He would admire them, his rooted students, and his words flowed over the plants blowing them kisses and gently patting them. The flowers seemed to understand, to stand up taller, to lift themselves skyward. Uncle Henry would look around at his garden and say, "I am sorry to do this, but you must come with me." Then he would pluck one small flower and place it into the buttonhole of his jacket. He wore it all day, lowering his head to periodically sniff it, whether there was a fragrance or not. As housekeeper #2 wandered around the kitchen completing morning duties, she peeked out the window and smiled as she watched the daily performance. They would notice each other, and the housekeeper would give a small wave; he would bow in greeting towards her. Their daily ritual.

The garden, the dominoes, the writing, kept Uncle Henry occupied during the days, but he silently suffered during the nights when the flowers could not be seen, the games were not being played, the ledger was not being filled with poems due to his shaking hands. He lived for the daylight; he dreaded the nighttime soreness, spasms, sufferings. But he took no relief from the small brown vials which gathered in the corner of his dresser drawer. There would come a proper time for their use.

He continued to write during the day, to offer his attempts at poetry for various family events. The older daughter's high school graduation party was an occasion for a special tribute whose beginning lines were:

> *So proud, so proud, we all are proud*
> *So let us sing her praises loud,*
> *She worked and studied through years of school,*
> *And proved to all, she was no fool.*

The poem went on in that way for about ten stanzas, and after a stunned moment, the G2 wife led the applause. Uncle Henry promised to write out the poem and give it to the daughter as a keepsake…his gift to her. The Professor became poet laureate of the household. Other affairs, circumstances, holidays received their own stanzas, all read by the professor, holding the green ledger, speaking in an increasingly raspy voice. The Fourth of July was greeted with a poem beginning with these lines:

> *The boom of the cannons, the screech of the guns,*
> *The marching of the soldiers in a line,*
> *Some bloodied from the battle,*
> *Some missing legs or eyes,*
> *Some shot in their thighs!*

Refrain:

> *Oh, the revolutionary heroes*
> *Who set our country free,*
> *We honor you this happy day.*
> *Claims him, Claims her, Claims me!*

The repeated refrain had gestures Uncle Henry had perfected. As he held the ledger in his right hand, he pointed with his left finger at various friends and neighbors who had gathered for the celebratory party. He would shout:

> *CLAIMS HIM* (point), *CLAIMS HER* (point),
> *CLAIMS ME* (points at himself followed by his thumb pushing his spectacles up closer to his eyes)

Those words would shoot up to the ceiling, all of them wearing spectacles which were falling halfway down the letters, sparkling and twinkling as if they were fireworks. It was something to behold. When the recitation of this poem was completed, the gathered crowd erupted into both laughter and applause, and the words from the poem and the noises from the audience scurried around together, shifting and flowing, wavering and roaming, attempting to fit into a ceiling or wall or woodwork. There was so much hubbub that many of the words and sounds needed to be escorted to the hallway or the kitchen where they could find a space to settle. Uncle Henry was so pleased with his performance that night, he took a small glass of the offered bootlegged beer. Prohibition may have been the law of the land, but on the Fourth of July, during the celebration of rebellion and freedom, it was not one which was staunchly followed.

The summer of 1928 turned to the autumn of 1928, and Uncle Henry's garden responded appropriately. I heard him as he whispered to himself about which flowers he would plant in order to create a colorful area from spring through late fall. His summer snapdragons and zinnias gave way to early fall's asters and celosia which made room for the cosmos and garden mums of late autumn. Henry would sometimes rest on an old wooden chair positioned by the garage facing the cinder alley, but after a while, he got up and continued his daily schedule: gardening in the morning, then resting, reading or writing at noon, resting, a visit with Jenkins on Wednesdays, then a rest, a small dinner, another check of the garden, reading or writing, and a nightly attempt at rebuffing the throes and throbs of increasing physical torment. Uncle Henry was no hero but he endured his agonies until it was not possible to do so any longer. I heard him during the nights as he moaned quietly, telling himself to choose a date, pick a time, come to closure. He did. Wednesday.

He was spending more time in his rooms, less time with the G2 family who were so involved with their own circumstances, they barely noticed when he did not come to dinner. Housekeeper #2 had recently become involved with a man from the neighborhood who worked at the nearby butcher shop, and between her duties at the house and this new beau, she didn't notice that she generally served only four, not five meals. The business activities of the G2 husband had him traveling for lunches and late meetings most days, and while he didn't pay much attention to Uncle Henry, the fact is he never really did. The wife had her luncheons and card parties and shopping trips which kept her busy much of the week, and while the younger daughter was still in school, the older daughter had taken a job in a shop downtown which meant she left early and came home late. Uncle Henry was alone most days. That suited him.

On Tuesday before the chosen date, he spent most of the day writing. He had sheets of paper upon which he wrote and crossed out, and wrote and revised, and finally seemed satisfied with what he had created. He carefully copied it into his frayed green ledger, using a new page for it, not bothering to continue writing on the partially used page which was his usual composing habit. He tore the original sheets containing the first drafts of the poem into small pieces and allowed them to fall into the corner trash bin. Then, as he was wont to do with newly written works, he read it aloud. And then he read it aloud once more, which is how I remember what he wrote. Frankly, I was astounded. I do not claim to know much about human poetry, but this seemed to me to be very different from the other things he had written. Different in a good way; it seemed a better effort. You will judge for yourself soon. He placed the ledger on the bookcase in the first room. It fell in back of some of the many books he had gathered there. I don't know if it was on purpose or a mistake; I am unsure he was even aware of what happened, and he never again wrote in the ledger or even looked for it. The green book containing the poetry and thoughts of the Professor had slipped down, in a space behind the built-in bookcase, in a spot which was exactly its size. It became lodged there, unseen, unnoticed. Even when the other books were removed and the shelf was dusted and wiped clean, there was no noticing it. No green was visible. It was concealed, obscured, undetected. It remains there even now, even after all these decades. It is the third secret.

Wednesday. Uncle Henry was very ill in the morning. He had little sleep that previous night. I listened to the whimpers and groans he attempted to stifle so as not to wake any of the family. He was more considerate of them with his dying than any of them were to him with their living. When he rose in the morning, he sat up and then rushed into the bathroom where he was sick. He drank a bit of water which did not stay down, and after being sick again, he looked at himself in the bathroom mirror, and spoke these words: "Well, look at you now. Not good for much more, ready to shuffle off, to take the next step. Are you brave enough?" and the words were weak and tiny, clinging to the walls and groping onto each other for help. They barely made it to a space where they collapsed, making no additional sounds.

He dressed himself, wrapped his scarf around his shoulders, made sure his socks matched, and combed back his hair which by now, barely covered his head. Although it was late morning, Henry gripped the banister as he went down the stairs and out to the backyard to see, once again, his garden. The steps he took were even and careful, and upon arriving there, he stood, the smallest of smiles on his face, and noted the colors which were autumn's offerings. There was a small yellow garden mum which had just bloomed, and he picked one of its flowers and whispered to it, "You will come with me." It was attached to the buttonhole in his jacket, and then he rewrapped the scarf tighter around his neck. He turned and looked at the kitchen for housekeeper #2 although he did not expect to see her since it was much later in the day, but she was there.

She looked out at him and waved. He bowed and waved back, something he did not usually do. She was unaware of the reason for the wave. It did not seem a *hello*. Housekeeper #2 smiled and held up a teacup, miming a question, asking if he wanted breakfast, but Uncle Henry just shook his head. "My, he is so thin. I wonder if he is ill?" she asked herself, and those words stood in the air next to her head looking inquisitively out at the man standing there before rushing up to the corner next to the tallest cabinet. The housekeeper put down the cup and continued to knead the bread she was making. She would not see him again until Jenkins called her attention to my front porch. Then she would realize what Uncle Henry's solitary wave meant.

It was Wednesday. The G2 family was gone to their various destinations; the housekeeper was baking bread and slicing vegetables for dinner; Jenkins was due in an hour, and Uncle Henry pulled himself back up the stairs to his room. He had arranged his things in order. Directions to the family were carefully written in a note which had been placed in the middle of the table. His few possessions were folded, packed, and placed in his suitcase and a bag. Both were on the floor next to the chair. He had removed the bedding, folded it and left it in the middle of the bed. All was in order. The only thing left to do was to remove the six small brown vials from the corner of the dresser drawer, pour the drops from each into the glass of water he had readied, and drink the concoction. He remembered the doctor's instructions because he repeated them to himself as he mixed the drops together.

"*Careful*, he said to me. *This is strong stuff.* Strong enough to harm me? I asked him. *Yes, if too much is taken.* Well, doctor, I hope you are correct," and those words presented themselves as strong words which surprised me. They were not hesitant at all as they walked steadily to the ceiling, staring down at the man who spoke them.

He closed his eyes and drank the liquid. I could tell it was not a pleasant taste, but he held his mouth shut and remained standing, his hands gripping the table until the drink settled in his stomach, staying there. He sighed, then glanced at the clock. It was a few minutes after twelve. Jenkins would come soon, ready to play Dominoes, anxious to walk to the diner for pie and coffee. His friend would find him at the front steps, would understand what had taken place. This was Uncle Henry's plan. I heard him speak it to himself regularly, as if to memorize what he would do. He looked once more around the room, and seeming assured that all was in order, he walked out to the stairway. Holding on to the banister, he placed one foot on each step, deliberately walking down them. At the front door, he stood for a moment, a bit unsteadily. He placed his hand on the doorknob, opened it, then stepped onto the porch, closing the door behind him. The day was sunny. It was one of those warm autumn days, when the summer season seems reluctant to disappear. He nodded at the sky. He sat on the second step on my porch and adjusted himself in the sun which poured its light onto his face. He wrapped the scarf around his neck once more, leaned down to smell the slight fragrance of the new yellow mum he had put in his buttonhole, and said to it, "Come, my yellow friend, we will travel to worlds unknown together." Then Uncle Henry, the Professor, placed his head against the concrete side of my porch, smiled up to the amenable warmth, and with a last slight sigh, closed his eyes.

Somewhat later than his appointed time, unusual for him, Jenkins came around the corner. When he saw Uncle Henry on my steps, he called out to him, "Professor, you are asleep in the sun. Wake up and allow me to beat you at your favorite game!" But Uncle Henry did not wake. There were no games played. Another human ending. Ah, well, perhaps Jenkins should have made the acquaintance of an Orange Roughy or a Greenland Shark.

Oh yes, that last thing he wrote. I admit to no knowledge of what is good or bad, or what type of poetry is better than others. I don't know that it matters. I simply know that the words he spoke, the form the poem took, the sense it made as he read what he wrote in that now hidden ledger, were different than any of the others. I claim no poetry expertise, but the meaning is clear. Those final spoken words rose, glimmering, sparkling, dazzling, up to the ceiling, not mixing with any of the other words written or spoken, remaining to themselves, luminous and radiant, immovable and motionless, yet filled with life. Judge for yourself:

> *Against brown, shingled wall the flowers grow*
> *And greet me daily in the early sun*
> *When I awake. To these bright things, I pose*
> *A wish: To view their colors when life's done.*
> *That time comes soon. The pain I suffer makes*
> *My ending clear. I know what I will do*
> *To hasten it along. I've stored what takes*
> *The aches away. I visit hurts anew*
> *Each day until I clamber down the stair*
> *And view that rainbowed plot. I dismiss pain*
> *And gather joy. The anguish I can bear*
> *Until the end when comfort I'll attain.*
> *I welcome darkness. Soon it comes for me.*
> *And with closed eyes, my flowered friends I'll see.*

10

Depressing Changes
(Mostly for the Humans)

So, Uncle Henry, poet and professor, made his decision and his departure. There might be something to be admired about that, a human attempt at subverting a human end. A grace note in the cacophony of human life music. Most likely, a justified fear of extended human pain. Whatever it was, Uncle Henry was gone. The note he left to the family instructed that his books and papers go to Jenkins, his outdated clothes sent to the needy, his body to the local funeral home where arrangements had been made (It was on Archer Avenue in a building whose brick front needed cleaning and tuckpointing, so I heard), and the small amount of money he had left was to be sent to a Mrs. Marjorie Andrews, whose address was listed as somewhere in Kansas City, Missouri. That last item caused quite a bit of family discussion. It was never discovered who she was or why he wanted to send her money (about fifty dollars), and Jenkins claimed he did not know and would not answer any of their questions. About six weeks after the letter with the money was sent, it was returned marked *Addressee Moved/Address Unknown*. The G2 family simply kept the money and purchased two new electric portable lamps for the house. They did not add any beauty to the tables where they were placed, and the light offered by them was dull.

For some weeks, there was a minor sadness which hung about my walls and bricks, but it dissipated rapidly as the G2 family soon resumed their daily activities and schedules. Uncle Henry's rooms were cleaned and settled, his few things removed, but the tattered green ledger remained hidden. The family did not think about renting the rooms out because money wasn't needed. At least not then. Because of the wealth made through a human devise called the Stock Market (I admit my lack of understanding of this despite the many words G2 husband spoke about it; however, I did appreciate the multitude of loud and seemingly strong words which attached themselves through the walls and into the bricks as he spoke regularly and thunderously into the desk telephone), plans were made for additional purchases. The first (unimportant to me) was G2 husband's desire to have a new automobile. He would gaze at the advertisements in the newspapers, reading bits and pieces aloud to the wife.

"Listen to this," and he would clear his throat and read in what was meant to be a theatrical tone, "*This new Model A is the Deluxe model…the car of the future. Car of the future* they say. Don't you think that is perfect for us? And the cost is a mere twelve hundred dollars."

"What!" and the wife looked up from her sewing and glared at him with a surprised look. "That is a ridiculous amount of money. What are you thinking?" and those words rose up with hands on their letters, shaking and stamping until they disappeared into the ceiling.

He sniffed and replied, "I am thinking we can afford that. We are better off, my dear, than you know. I want a new car and will order one. I'm just deciding which one I want," and he continued to turn the pages of the paper.

"*My dear,*" and the wife herself sniffed, "You have never called me that, and now you do? Humph. Putting on airs."

There was a quiet for a time and some mumbling came from the man, but nothing was said until another page was turned, and he spoke again. "THIS is the one. It is perfect. Chrysler has a new automobile: the Imperial 80. Listen to this: the car is *as fine as money can build,* and it is *Justly the choice of those who know the finest.* What do you think of that?" and he continued to read.

"What is THAT cost? Fifteen hundred dollars, I suppose," and she didn't even look up, thinking that cost was absurd. When there was no answer, she looked up and asked again.

"Well, it says this car is *for the sophisticated owner,* and that is me. Actually, that is us, right?"

She stared at him. "How much?"

He cleared his throat and swallowed. "Well, you can get one for $3595, but there is also a model for $2495. And before you yell, I am telling you we can afford this. In fact, I am going to make some calls tomorrow and see if there is one available. This is the one for us. Look at how perfect it is. Can't you picture yourself in it?" and he held up the page with the ad and hid behind it. When there was no answer, he peeked around at his wife who was looking at the ad, but saying nothing. She went back to her sewing and said nothing the remainder of the day. However, my walls and ceiling and woodwork shivered with anticipation of what might be said.

The following day, G2 husband spent a couple hours on the telephone in his office, calling around to various car dealers wanting to see what was available. Alas, the Chrysler Imperial 80 was not readily available, even at the ridiculous cost he was willing to pay, and he had to settle on placing his name on a waiting list with the car promised sometime in the fall of 1929. That was not to happen. Instead, he spent some of his riches by replacing the wireless radio set he had with the new Philco table model and console which he put into the front room next to the bay window. "How much was that?' inquired the wife. He told her it was less than one hundred dollars, and completely affordable. I knew he paid about twice that amount. But the family appeared to enjoy it more than they would have the new and expensive car. The old Model T continued to be driven.

The second item was much more important. Plans were being made to finally complete me. The garden apartment was going to be built. The feeling of being incomplete would be gone, and I waited impatiently for the results which I understood, at least according to the conversations which I paid close attention to, would take about six months. It took much longer than that. Years, in fact. It turned out two things kept the apartment from being completed. The first was the lack of supplies and difficulty getting workers. The second thing was a wedding.

The older daughter was getting married. Through his business interactions, the G2 husband met and dealt with a business owner from the near-north side, and he and his son, who was learning the business, came to dinner a few times. Once the son met the older daughter, they began to *keep company*, as it was called. The two continued to see each other, and by the end of 1928, love was declared and a wedding was planned. All thoughts of spending money on either a new car or my garden apartment were forgotten. Apparently, the sort of wedding that was wanted cost money, and that is where it went.

"Those things can wait for a while," argued the wife, "Your daughter's wedding is more important. And we need to begin planning and organizing it. This will take money, and the car and garden apartment can wait until after the June wedding."

The husband was hesitant to do this, but eventually agreed. Then, he discovered the wedding cost. I heard him mutter to himself that he had the money to do it all, but when he looked at the papers and ledger books on the desk, he made a strange movement with his mouth and whispered "Damn it" under his breath. *Damn it* was heard often through the early months of 1929, and occurred so frequently during the latter months that they formed their own group, alternately snarling and weeping. A pack of worddogs, positioned in the woodwork above the office desk, keeping all other words at bay. There was reason enough for their existence as it turned out.

A smaller party was held earlier that spring when the younger daughter graduated from high school, and more money was spent. I was concerned. Listening to the G2 husband mutter over his books and bills, it seemed to me that the amount of available funds spent on things such as food and clothing and presents was going to prevent my basement from being completed. Human wants were superseding my needs.

The wedding was much more elaborate than expected with discussions and arguments about fashion, flowers, and something called photography taking place daily. During the morning breakfast, at the dinner table, in the evenings, and particularly on the weekends, the G2 mother and daughters spoke, at times quite loudly, about what should be planned and ordered. Words were plentiful, and as they rose from their mouths, they took on various shapes and colors. Gold was often mentioned by the daughters as a popular color scheme for the wedding, but the mother preferred various shades of pink. The words took on their colors as they gathered together above the heads of the women. The curlicue letters wandered in and out of each other, creating patterns, mixing the words, changing to darker shades as the conversations grew louder. Periodically the older daughter would burst into tears and run from the dining room or front parlor, slamming the bedroom door as the words which were garbled from her lips followed her, pushing each other out of the way, wetness forming around them as they cried along with their maker. These discussions were useless to me. Wet words do not make for strong support and do not last longer than a year or two. I was glad when a compromise was reached: gold with bits of light pink in the enormous bouquet of flowers both the bride and her sister would carry were finally ordered, along with shorter vases of flowers for tables at the luncheon reception, and tall vases to decorate the front of the church. Smaller bouquets for various women and boutonnieres for the men were ordered. When the G2 husband received this bill, the oath *Damn it* rang throughout the house, causing the other and smaller *damns* to shiver and the G2 wife to stand at the front of the desk, hands on her hips, staring at the man until he slumped over in his chair, and mumbled *sorry* in such a weak voice that the word disappeared before it could reach a wall.

When the wedding was over and the parties were ended, I was relieved, but that relief was not to last. The married daughter was moving out. She and her new husband were living with his parents on the north-side so he could be closer to their business. As her belongings and some furniture were being moved from my basement, a terrible thing happened: one of my basement windows was broken in the move. I felt a shock as the splintered glass fell to the floor, the crashing sound thrown to a side wall, sliding across the cement floor, snaking up an opposite wall, the discordant sound jangling there, harsh and brassy, disturbing all the other words, some of them, the bravest ones, peeking out to see the horror. Oh, I can hear you laughing, thinking: *this is only a small thing, a broken window, a tiny issue.* Consider your own human body: a broken arm, a smashed leg, a dislocated collarbone. Do you feel the pain? It is the same for me. Well, almost. I watched as the glass was swept up, thrown into the large garbage pail in the cinder alley, two boards carelessly hammered into place across the open sore, a superficial band-aid; darkness filling in the space where once light had been.

"Don't worry", commented the G2 husband, "that can be easily fixed. Now, lift up that end of the table and let's try to not break this other window."

Humans: careless and stupid.

So, the older daughter moved out, but hers was not the only wedding. No, it was not the younger daughter. She didn't have a beau and had few friends, except for housekeeper #2. During the summer months of 1929, the two of them often spoke together in the kitchen, the younger daughter watching the work, sometimes helping with the tasks, and asking questions of the housekeeper. *Why do you add salt to the bread mixture? How did you learn to iron those shirts without burning yourself? Are the potato eyes poisonous?* The questions-words and their answer-words stayed together as they wandered into the corners of the kitchen, to the wooden baseboards, to the painted walls. They clung closely, the questions and answers, like a teacher with students, the answers looking up expectantly at the questions. I listened to the humans talk, and heard about housekeeper #2's plans for a marriage.

"How exciting! Congratulations! When will it be? Does my mother know? How many people will be there? What does your dress look like?"

The housekeeper didn't answer for a time. She stopped the kneading of the bread and looked out the window before sighing such a desperate sigh that the sound grew larger as it lifted upwards. She wiped her hands and covered the dough before looking at daughter #2.

"Won't be a wedding like your sister's. Can't afford that, you know. Not everyone has the money this family does. I will talk to your mother today. I told her yesterday that I needed to speak with her about some things, and when she returns from her shopping trip, I'll tell her. I need next Monday morning free. We are going to City Hall in the morning with my best friend and her husband, and my new mother-in-law, and the wedding will only take about fifteen minutes. We plan on going to a late breakfast afterwards at a nearby diner, and I'll be back here at work about one in the afternoon. My best dress is fine to wear."

The daughter appeared shocked. "Oh. I guess that will still be exciting for you. After all, you will be married then. Wait…does that mean you won't work for us after that? Is that part of what you will tell Mother?"

"I hope to still work here for a while, although I won't sleep here. My new husband rented a small house, and I'll be there with him. Not sure how long I will work here since I will have my own place to care for, and I need to let your mother know that once a family starts, I'll be gone."

The daughter nodded her head, saying, "Well, I am glad you will still be here. I would miss you. And a family is sometime in the future, so maybe you will be here for a long time."

There was some hesitancy on the housekeeper's part before she admitted, "Won't be that long. Just a few months," and the look she gave the daughter was a side-glance, and even I understood what was meant. The smile faded from the daughter's face as she seemed to grasp the meaning and her cheeks took on a rosy color.

"Oh," she said in a small voice, and could not help but glance at the front of the housekeeper's apron where there appeared a tiny bulge. Her cheeks turned a darker pink and an additional *Oh* from her lips rose up, colored in the same pinkish hue. There was quiet for a short time, and then the daughter said, "I am happy for you, and I hope things work out. Now, do you want me to help with those vegetables? I really have nothing else to do right now."

Together, the two of them worked in the kitchen until the G2 wife returned from her trip. The daughter excused herself to go for a walk while the necessary conversation took place. Housekeeper #2 explained her situation, and it was *blah blah blah* this and *blah blah blah* that until both the wife and the housekeeper ended in tears which, as I have explained before, are not particularly useful in strengthening my walls and bricks. Soggy words accompanied by wetness floated up from the two humans, intertwining and meshing and twisting until they combined into one translucent teardrop which hung resplendently from the edges of the dining room wall and slowly dematerialized. The housekeeper could stay until the end of the summer when she would no longer be of service to the G2 family. She agreed to help find someone new to take her place by the middle of October. Her wages would remain the same although she would no longer sleep at the house. Neither woman was completely satisfied with the arrangement, but neither was completely dissatisfied with it either.

Changes happened: marriages, moving, and most especially, money. In September of 1929, G2 husband sat one evening reading the *Chicago Tribune's* Business Section as the wife read through *The Ladies Home Journal.* The husband let out a sound which was part snort and part laugh, causing the wife to stare up at him.

"Something interesting?" she asked.

"Well, this man, a Roger Babson, gave a speech and proclaimed that a crash is coming. He said: *A crash is coming and it may be terrific.* He says also…investors should *get out of debt.* Hmm."

"Is he right? Are you worried?"

The husband continued to read before he answered, "Well, I suppose it could happen, but the *Tribune* seems to think not. And President Hoover says the market is sound. Don't worry. I'm sure it is nothing," but I noticed he scrunched his lips to the side and furrowed his brows in further thought, and his words, leaving his lips, were uncertain and hesitant as they stared about them, unsure of what to do. The wife went back to her magazine article. Later that night, I watched as the husband sat at his desk, shifting papers, reading through the newspaper again, working with a pencil and figuring out some numbers. He seemed distressed. The following day, he left the house early in the morning.

When he returned, he pushed open my front door, peered around to see if anyone was near, and quietly entered the front parlor where he stood still for a time. The wife and daughter were out in the backyard with the housekeeper, and once he heard their chatter softly drifting in through the open kitchen window, he let out a small sigh which crawled to the top of his head and waited there until another small sigh met it. The husband walked rapidly to his bedroom and shut the door. I watched as he took a thick envelope from his inside coat pocket, another from his jacket pocket, and a third which was stuffed into his trouser pocket. This last one he dropped, and money spilled out. He quickly picked it up, shoved it back into the envelope and produced a rubber band which he wrapped around the three envelopes. He hurriedly pushed the banded pack into the bottom drawer of his bureau under some pajamas and a winter scarf. He shut the drawer, then opened it again and rearranged everything so that it looked undisturbed. No, Reader, this is not another hidden secret. The money was used through the following year. I have no idea how much was there, but eventually it was all used up. No secret stash would be found in that drawer.

Roger Babson, as it turned out, was correct. I don't know exactly what a *stock market crash* is, but I saw the effects of it on the G2 family, and I will admit, that crash appeared to do more damage than the crash from my basement's broken window. Which, I will remind you, was, unfairly to me, not repaired for years. Unfortunately, for the humans, the G2 husband lost his business and most of his money. "We must tighten our belts around here!" he shouted at the wife when she came home from a shopping trip loaded with packages containing a new winter hat, new dresses, and two boxes filled with new shoes. "Take those things back. No more shopping. No more parties. No more restaurant reservations! No more even thinking about a new car!" Those words scrambled out of his mouth in oversized black letters and rose menacingly to the ceiling where other words peeked out from various spaces, wondering what the new commotion was. "No spending! Do you understand?" The wife, tears cascading down her cheeks, turned and went into their bedroom where she sat on the bed and sobbed. Eventually the husband calmed down and went in to speak with her.

"I'm sorry, but you don't understand how serious this is. I don't have the business. The banks are closing. We have lost almost everything, and I'm unsure what will happen. No one really knows," and he sat next to her and wrapped an arm around her shoulders.

"I'll return all this tomorrow," she said, and took out her handkerchief to wipe her eyes. "I just thought these were such a good buy that it was a shame to pass up a bargain."

The husband shook his head slowly. "We can't afford to get new things right now. Everything is in chaos, and we have to wait and see what happens in the next few weeks. I think this can be cleared up quickly, and I'm hoping I will be able to recoup some cash and maybe start again. The government can't allow this to go on for a long time. But in the meanwhile, we will need to be careful with what we spend."

The wife nodded. "Fine. But the housekeeper is gone, and I haven't replaced her yet. How will we pay the new one?"

There was a tense quietness, and when the husband answered, "We won't. We can't. For at least a few weeks, the housework will have to fall on your shoulders, and our daughter will need to help." Tears started again.

The weeks turned into months, then years, and I heard from the old red-brick to my north and the yellow-brick to my south that their humans had the same troubles. The problems seemed to be city wide, but then, as I heard the newspaper reports read out loud, it was country wide, and even most parts of the world seemed to suffer from whatever had befallen this country. There were many changes, not happy ones, for the G2 family. The money in the envelopes the husband had stored away helped to support them for a time, but it did not last. Slowly, the husband's hope that the financial crisis would pass quickly, faded.

For the next few months, he would drive the car to his old office because the building was still open. There was nothing for him to do there, according to the wife, and she complained about his traveling. Those trips did not continue once the building itself was closed down and offered for sale. When he was eventually forced to stay home, the husband would sit at his home office, reading through old files, making phone calls which always seemed to end unhappily, reading the newspapers again and again. After a time, he ignored the desk area and sat in a chair he had moved to the window in the front parlor, and stared out at the traffic which traveled the boulevard. He started to read a book, but never seemed to get beyond a page or two before he let it bump on the floor, causing a sound between a *squish* and an *ouch* which startled the smaller words sequestered near the ceiling. The husband grew quieter and thinner and gloomier. After a time, the most consistent noise heard from him were coughs whose squawky utterings rose to the top of the ceiling, wrapping themselves around the plaster roses which years before were created by the Irish workman and his son. The wife fared no better. She had to replace her shopping trips with standing in line at the grocery store, her restaurant meals with simple meals made in her own kitchen, her theater tickets with listening to the Philco radio at night while darning socks and sewing on buttons. She wore the same hats and coats from year to year, and could not renew her subscription to *The Ladies Home Journal*. She grew quiet too, but in a different way than the husband. Anger and worry consumed her, and she mumbled under her breath while dusting and sweeping and washing the family's socks and underwear. The G2 husband and wife were not the same humans who moved into me years before, but it was the younger daughter who was most surprising.

She was eighteen when her high school years were completed, and although she talked about continuing her education to become a teacher, the crash put an end to that. Instead, after months of listening to her parents quarrel about money, clash over shopping trips, bicker about jobs, argue about household tasks, she stepped in and spoke to her parents as if she were the parent, they the children. The G2 husband and wife were startled and surprised, but, amazingly, paid attention to her.

Her words rose from her lips in a straight, competent line. "The two of you need to cease arguing. We need to work together if we're going to get through this, and I have ideas and plans. We need to have a strict budget because there is almost no money, and no one seems to know how long this mess will last. We will, all of us, complete the household jobs together. Mother, Dad is right…no more shopping trips. Dad, Mother is right…you need to do more than just sit and look out the window. So, here is what we will do…" and she informed them about the plans, instructed them as to their tasks.

She was fair about the household work, taking on most of it herself. She generated needed money by selling extra furniture and household items, finding businesses willing to purchase them and doing the bargaining herself. Extra furniture was sold for *practically nothing*, as the wife complained, and despite the tears and disagreements, the wife's jewelry, the baubles she was so fond of wearing, went the way of the furniture. When more money was needed, the home office: the desk, the chair, the side table and cabinet, was sold. Despite the husband's arguments and forbiddances, the daughter made him understand that the items were no longer used or needed, and certainly, could be replaced once times improved. He, muttering quietly, relented, sitting again in his chair, staring out the window, coughing in resignation. She wanted to sell the car, but the father claimed it would only be done *over my dead body*. The car, rarely used despite the availability of gasoline, remained in my garage. There was no place for the G2 husband to travel. Meals were simple, but, under the mindful care of the daughter, prepared with attention. The years of watching and helping the housekeeper with her kitchen tasks paid off, and the daughter taught her mother how to make the recipes she had written down. Bread was baked, and dishes were washed. Laundry was sorted, and cleaning was completed. Yard work duties were shared, and winter snow was shoveled from the front steps. Garbage was removed. Shopping lists were made and adhered to, and while arguing and bickering and quarreling never completely ceased, the times spent doing it decreased. As the depressing years continued, I watched and listened and formed a grudging admiration for the younger daughter, even though my basement window remained broken and boarded up.

Meal planning, food preparation, and grocery shopping seemed to take up most of the day for the G2 family. While the daughter, and sometimes her mother went grocery shopping two or three times a week, there were long lines and few choices. At least those were the main complaints heard from the mother. After a while, in an attempt to cut costs and provide fresh food, the daughter began a vegetable garden in the space Uncle Henry had planted his flowers. The first attempt was not very successful, but the second attempt saw the vegetable production greatly improved. The father was put in charge of daily weeding and watering, and the daughter taught him how to pick the vegetables when they were ripe enough. At first, he complained and quibbled about this new task.

"I'm not a farmer, I'm a businessman. Why can't you or your mother do this?" and the words stormed from his mouth to the branches of the yard's one tree, staring down angrily at the daughter and the vegetable patch before rushing to the bricks at my back where they pushed past each other.

"Mother and I are working too. You sit staring out the front window too often. This fresh air and sunshine are good for you. I hear that coughing, and you need to move more. Besides, I'm familiar with your capabilities, and know you can be two things at the same time: a good businessman and a good farmer. Isn't that correct?" Those soothing words caressed the father's arms and face and lifted slowly into the air, hovering around him, mellowing him out, calming him down. He shrugged his shoulders and began the weeding, while the daughter bent over to brush his cheek with hers. She had a way with both of her parents. Her words were always delicate and benign, mollifying the parents, calming and comforting them, just as a parent might deal with a small child. She would have been a good teacher, I suppose.

The father took to his duties, working in the garden, pulling up mostly weeds, stacking the ready vegetables in the basket the daughter provided, straightening up only when he had to cough. For a long time, the garden helped to provide ingredients for the soups and stews the family lived on, and the G2 husband worked consistently, although somewhat grudgingly, at the gardening until the day he leaned over to pluck a ripe tomato and fell over, smashing the one ripe and a second unripe tomato into the ground, grinding them into the sweater he had taken to wear that morning. He had been coughing often and looking pale despite the daily sun and fresh air. He was not young, and it was bound to happen. I watched as he lay there, breath slowly escaping from his throat, dirt covering the side of his face. In a while, there was no more breath. Only dirt. And the mash of the red tomatoes. Sometime later, the G2 wife looked out the kitchen window, screamed, and rushed out to help up the husband she thought had only fallen, but discovered there was no breath left in his body.

The car was sold to pay for his funeral. *Over my dead body*, I recalled him saying. If I had been able to chuckle at that, I might have. So, the husband was buried and the wife mourned by staying in bed each day until noon, offering little help with household chores. For a while, the older daughter and the young son she and her husband had produced, came and stayed with the wife and younger daughter. The two daughters discussed what to do now that their father was gone and their mother was useless.

"Sell this place," said the older daughter. "It is too large for the two of you. I am sure my husband can find a small house or apartment for you in our neighborhood. Besides, I could use mother's help with this one since the new baby is coming soon," and she pulled the child away from the counter as he reached for a knife. "Now that times are not so difficult, I'll bet there is a job for you in the family business. We were lucky to keep it through these years, and I would love to have you closer to us too. My husband said that the government is doing something to help the housing market and loans will be easier to get. This house will sell fast. I am sure of it."

The daughters tried to interest their mother in some future plans, but she was indifferent to their recommendations. She told them to do what was necessary, that she just didn't care and would agree to whatever was decided. Her words were somber and despondent. They curled around her in doleful and downcast clumps, their color shades of gray, and spread slowly through the bedroom walls, languishing in discouraged groups. And the daughters did exactly as they planned.

In the spring of 1938, a large truck pulled up in front of me and the boxes which the daughters had packed and stored around my walls were carried into the back of it. The furniture which had not been sold was also packed. Only the large dining table and chairs had been left. "Too large to fit in the apartment and too good to throw away. The next family can use it," commented the younger daughter. The moving took only a few hours. The older daughter had come by earlier in the morning to pick up her mother who said she could not stay to watch the house being emptied because it was too heartbreaking. The younger daughter and her brother-in-law supervised the loading of the truck and the movement of the boxes. Then my front door was locked; the loaded truck left, and the younger daughter sat in the car which would take her to the small north-side apartment where she and her mother would live. She had already begun her new job in the office at the brother-in-law's business, and she said she was anxious to get settled, to begin a new life. As they drove away, the younger daughter's head was turned to watch me. I think a tear was running down her cheek. Maybe not.

For the first time, there were no humans in me. I was empty.

11

Empty. For a While.

Empty.

For many decades, I had humans in me. Around me. Outside of me. In the yard, in the garage, on the walkway. Sitting on the front steps and sometimes on the back ones. Upstairs in the rooms at the top and downstairs near the garden apartment space and the storage area. Certainly on the main floor: the parlor, the dining room, the bedrooms, the kitchen and indoor bathrooms. All over me. Sometimes only one, other times two, maybe even five or more humans. Humans who were talking, laughing, shouting, weeping, singing, making noises and sounds which supported my bricks and walls and woodwork. For decades. I can hear you thinking: *The red-brick house missed the humans. Their sounds and noises and emotions were gone. The emptiness must have been a shock for it.* This is what you, the reader, think, what you believe.

You are wrong.

It was delightful not to hear the human babel and bluster. To hear only the sounds made by me: some creaking, a little grating, perhaps a rumbling or clinking. Think of the sounds your body makes, often without any conscious effort on your part. I was relaxed and pleased. I welcomed the absence of human noises, the absence of human smells, the absence of human touches. It was restful. I had no problems. If I wanted to entertain myself, there were plenty of sounds and noises and emotions to release, to hear anytime I wished. And sometimes, I would.

There was the time I loosed the words from the Robert Richardson years: *security, pride, uniform, marching, training, rifles, and death.* As they came forward, they once again arranged themselves in two straight lines with *death* in the front. They moved in formation around my space, weaving through each other, creating booming, threatening sounds as they grew larger, and then, after a time, I returned them to their spot. *Death* was stubborn, and I needed to force it into the space with the others. More than once, I took out the gentle words of husband #2's sister. I took pleasure in the phrases describing the spring daffodils, the summer snap-dragons, the fall mums. The words came out into the air and formed a wreath. They danced in a circle, and I was content. When they found their spaces once again in the wall and bricks, they remained polite while reentering. No pushing. No shoving. The larger words helped the smaller ones, and they quietly murmured and I pretended they gave off a pleasing floral scent which, had I the ability to smell, I would have enjoyed. This was one of my favorite activities.

I remained alone and empty and then, one late afternoon, my front door was unlocked, and two men entered. One was the G2 brother-in-law. The other was a stranger who held a notebook and pen and as they walked through my rooms and talked, wrote things down.

"Well," the stranger commented, "a pleasant appearing parlor. How many bedrooms?"

"There are two large ones and a smaller one off the kitchen. Two rooms are upstairs, and a bathroom is on each floor."

The stranger jotted some words in the notebook as he nodded his head. "Fine. And the downstairs is not yet made into a garden apartment?"

"No, although there is some framing for the rooms. We can go downstairs and see what is there. Do you want to go upstairs first?"

"Yes, after we finish this floor," and they walked into the dining room. "Is the dining table and chairs to be sold with the house?"

"It can be, since it was not needed for the small apartment. Is that a problem?"

"No," replied the stranger, "we will just advertise it as such."

Sold? That was news to me. Of course, I assumed other humans would be moving in, but it wasn't until I actually heard the word that I realized why these men were here. They continued walking through me, talking and making notes. Their words wore business suits and hats and looked around, examining the walls and woodwork before disappearing into them. After examining my interior, the men walked around my back yard and went into the garage as the man with the pencil and pad furiously wrote. They walked through me once more, went out my front door, locked it, and stood talking on my porch.

"We will advertise it and start showing it to potential buyers in a few weeks. Cleaning should be done, and I have a company that will do it. I think the broken basement window should be repaired as soon as possible. Do you want me to take care of it or do you want to do it? It will be cheaper if you take care of it."

"I can arrange for the replacement," said the brother-in-law, "It should be done this week."

FINALLY! It was both satisfying to hear and aggravating it took so long, but I would be repaired. The two men went down my steps, shook hands, and left. A couple days later, my basement window was replaced by some workmen who spoke a language which I had not heard before. Their words and work noises flew into the surrounding window frame and bricks, segregating themselves from the familiar words which had poked out to view the goings-on. For some time, the two word-groups stared at each other, but there was no trouble between them, and they eventually settled back into their separate spaces. Later that week, other humans came to clean my walls and floors, make my windows shiny, buff my woodwork. Finally, the original stranger came through once again, made additional notes, and a sign: HOUSE FOR SALE, was pounded into my front lawn. The parade through me began.

And now, for some complaints. TRUTHFUL and OBVIOUS, but really, you humans are so disrespectful of me, of houses in general. Some of the potential "buyers" brought their children with them, and had I been able to do something about those tiny, sticky, dirty hands touching my walls and woodwork (just cleaned!), those small feet stamping around my floors leaving bits and pieces of leaves and dirt there (also just wiped and washed), those squeaky high-pitched voices crying and screeching into my walls, shoving the other words and emotions back and away from them, believe me, I would have. I understand the need for these tiny creatures as replacements for those humans who die, but they are maddening and agitating and disagreeable none the less. I feared that I would be inhabited by a human group containing these wildlings, but that was not the case. Or so I believed.

The next group to inhabit me will be known as the G3 family. At first there was an older couple, husband and wife, who viewed me twice. I listened as they told the stranger, who I realized was put in charge of selling me, that their son would also be living with them, and they would bring him the next time. I feared their son was a child, but when they returned, they brought a human male who was obviously grown. They all walked to my basement to view my unfinished garden apartment space, and as I listened to their plans, a feeling of excitement invaded my area.

"Well, I think we can make a four-room apartment here," and the G3 father walked through the space, eyeing the boards and the walls, looking out the high windows, opening and closing the side door which would be used as the apartment's entrance. He turned to the other man and explained, "My son and I work in the construction business, and this is something we can work on together. Look," and he pointed to some pipes which were placed against my far wall, "this is set up so that a bathroom can be placed here, then the kitchen and a bedroom. There," and he pointed towards the front, "will be the front parlor and another bedroom over here. This will work, don't you think?"

The son nodded. He walked to the south wall and motioned with his hands. "A wall right here will separate the apartment from this storage area. We can build additional shelves for storage there, and in about six months, if we work nights and weekends, we can get it done."

More discussion took place, and I must admit, I was beginning to almost tolerate this new group. Then plans were made to visit once more and this time, bring the G3 son's wife to view the place. There was no mention of children, so I held out a hope there would be none. But, during the next visit, when the entire G3 group came, I saw that the son's wife had a suspicious bump on her front. This was the same bump the former housekeeper #2 had. It contained a new human, a baby, a squalling and crying tiny thing who would grow to contain tiny sticky dirty hands, muddy shoes, and piercing screams which would invade my space for months, for years. My hopes for quiet humans were ruined.

It took a while, but they moved in. At first it was just the older parents who brought in boxes and furniture, setting things around, moving dishes and pans into kitchen shelves, plugging in the lamps and adjusting their shades, making the bedroom off the front parlor their own. Then the son and his wife and her bump came with their boxes. They set up the second bedroom as theirs, ordered their clothes in the closet and the bureau, installed a mirror over a small dressing table and stool, fashioned the dried flowers from a wedding bouquet on top of the bureau. The four of them went to the small bedroom off the kitchen and stood looking around it.

"Perfect for a nursery, don't you think?" asked the young wife with the bump. "This needs to be painted, but I just don't know about the color. What should it be?"

Both men shrugged their shoulders, but the older wife said, "Yellow, a soft yellow would be nice, and it will be perfect for either a boy or a girl."

"I suppose. And the coverlet I saw at the store had polka dots of yellow in it," and the young wife patted her bump and smiled as her words rose up, a soft yellow color emanating from them.

The walls were painted; the coverlet was purchased; a baby bed, a *crib,* was set up, and the family, all four of them and the bump, settled into me. Eventually the boxes were emptied and the furniture adjusted. Once again, I oriented myself to humans with their words, their noises, their smells. My walls and bricks and wood, the ceilings and floors and windows began to fill with their conversations, emotions, and noises. When eventually the bump turned into a baby, its snuffling and crying and whining and fussing, the babbling and gurgling sounds, all, lifted up softly into the spaces, gently handled by the words and sounds already there who allowed them to cuddle and cling. I doubted their ability to strengthen the walls and bricks and windows, but assumed that the sheer number of them would be useful, and I gradually became used to these annoying odd sounds.

And again, humans disappointed me. Slowly, work was started on my garden apartment, but when the men came home from their day jobs, they were tired and often put off doing additional work. Some weekends were filled with the noise of hammering and sawing and yelling, and I was glad for both the strengthening noises and the work which was accomplished. But it was not enough, and when the bump turned into the baby, the hammering and sawing and yelling practically ceased so that the baby could sleep, so it would not be disturbed. Whispers and tip-toeing took the place of sawing and hammering, and the expected six months passed. My basement remained in an unfinished state.

And money. Another human issue. The cost of completing the apartment was more than expected. The cost of that baby was too, and when extra shifts were offered at the young husband's job, he took them, working longer hours and sleeping at weird times. The hammering and sawing mostly stopped because not only the baby needed quiet to sleep, but so did the young husband. Apparently, there were two babies in the house. Murmuring, muttering, mumbling took the place of actual conversation, and as these undertones and sighings crawled weakly and reservedly up my walls, I doubted they would add much to the strengthening of them. Delays, difficulties, and discouragements.

It was the older wife who decided that renting out the upper rooms would help bring in needed cash. "I think some other owners did that. There is no reason we can't," she claimed. The rooms were recleaned; cheap furniture was brought and settled in the spaces, and a small Kelvinator refrigerator was placed in the corner of the first room, next to the bookcase. It was decided that while no meals would be offered, limited kitchen privileges would be allowed. A sign was placed in the window, and eventually the rooms were, once again, in use. This G3 group had no experience in being landlords, so there were difficulties and problems with the men who rented the rooms. They didn't keep up with the defrosting of the Kelvinator, and left dirty dishes in the kitchen. It took months for the issues to be worked out, but eventually, the older wife figured out what to do and how to do it. There were times I longed for the organization and common sense of the sister of husband#2 from years before, but she was long gone, and her useful ledger lost. And then another bump appeared on the young wife, and a second baby necessitated the younger couple's move to their own house some blocks away. (I heard it was cheaply made using something called asbestos to support the concrete and pipes and walls.) But when they moved, the babies were gone, and there were not limitations on making noise. The young husband came back periodically, to help his father complete the garden apartment. It took much longer than they thought to finish it, but at least work was being done.

I'll hurry this along for readers because it is, frankly, boring. Another war occurred, but the rooms upstairs continued to be rented. There were often new renters, all men, and few stayed longer than several months. None of the men left any hidden secrets. Dirty socks, old newspapers, and a refrigerator in need of cleaning and defrosting were the calling cards left. Time moved, and the young couple's babies grew larger and noisier, bringing their sticky hands with them when they visited, and later, as they played with a ball in my back yard, I worried about protecting my windows. Blah and blah. There is little to tell except for two major incidents. The first is that my basement apartment, after much too much time, was FINALLY finished, and a couple moved in bringing their own furniture with them. They were older with no children. I was grateful for that. That's all I will say about them due to their lackluster lives and characterless existence. Their conversations, simple and common, just barely supported my walls in the garden apartment. So much for them. The second incident happened some years after that second war. Because of the issues and troubles with the men who rented my upstairs rooms, the G3 wife decided a woman might not be so careless with the furniture, the kitchenware, and the Kelvinator; she would keep the rooms reasonably clean. But it was a while until a woman knocked on my front door and inquired about the rooms for rent. She was brought into the dining room, offered a cup of coffee, and interviewed as to her background, financial ability, and reason for needing the rooms.

She answered the personal questions carefully, logically, sincerely. The following week, after the first month's rent was paid, Mrs. Charles (Ellen) Shaw took up residence in my upstairs.

Despite her careful and logical answers to the G3 wife's inquiries, they were not all, as I suspected, sincere. You had to expect that, didn't you? Her real story was sad, sorry to spoil the surprise, and she was the one who left the fourth secret in me. It remains hidden in the far corner of the upstairs hallway linen closet, tucked into the upper shelf, fallen into a cracked spot on the wall, not seen, unused, a sorrowful reminder that human lives are often…hmm…messy.

12

Mrs. Charles (Ellen) Shaw, 1955

Insincerity and lying run parallel paths. But sometimes they do intersect. Humans can be insincere. Humans often are liars. Don't take offense, reader, you know this. Your insincerity/lies vary according to the purpose, the type, the company. I know this because I have listened to the humans in me for decades. The men boarders sincerely promised the G3 wife to live according to her rules, but they lied. They drank liquor from the bottles hidden under the bed and the top of the bookcase. They smoked with their heads hanging out the upstairs windows, flicking their cigarettes on my lawn and walk. They invented reasons for not having their rent on time, claiming their pay had been stolen or the manager failed to pass out their salary when in fact, they had spent it drinking or gambling or taking some woman to that hotel on thirty-fifth street, the one with the dirty yellow bricks, the split wooden sign, the broken walkways. (I know about it because other buildings and the streets spread the news.) And humans talk to each other on the walkways and sidewalks, on my porch, in the cinder alley (And I get much of my knowledge from that alley who is never quiet.) But mostly, humans talk to themselves when they are alone. I discover their insincerity, their lies, their secrets.

However, it's difficult to correctly label Mrs. Shaw as either insincere or a liar. For one thing, she rarely talked aloud to herself, so I could not hear her truths. For another, she did not spend as much time in me as other renters because she had two jobs. If she had been around more often, I suspect she would have spoken aloud to herself just as the others had. She did sometimes, and I was able to understand her whispered words which, like compact, cramped containers, crept to the ceiling. Overall, she was fairly quiet, and what I did know about her I have gathered from her few words, her actions, and the information spread by the buildings and streets who are my neighbors. We speak in a non-human way, through our special methods, sharing warnings and particulars, and, I suppose, the truthful word is *gossip*. Gossip about the humans who abide in us, who walk on us, on the walkways and sidewalks and streets. We are eyes without human eyes and mouths without human mouths, but I assume, if you have read this far, you have come to that understanding. Much of what I believe about Mrs. Shaw and her life is based on what I have been told, based on the few conversations she had with others, based on her actions, based on her occasional self-whispers. It started with her interview with the G3 wife. I have drawn conclusions about her sincerity. Draw your own.

"Mrs. Shaw, I hope you don't mind a few questions."

"Of course not."

"I guess I would like to know about *Mr.* Shaw," and she looked pointedly at Ellen's left hand which did not contain a wedding band.

Ellen Shaw saw her glance at the empty left hand, nodded her head, and sighed. "Mr. Shaw, Charles, was lost during the war. I sold my wedding band to help out my family."

A sound like a combination of a sigh and a moan left the G3 wife's lips as she slowly shook her head. "I am so sorry, dear. We lost so many good, decent men during the war. Please accept my condolences."

(Just a few honest questions here. What was meant by Mrs. Shaw's use of the word *lost*? Lost in the sense of *dead*? Or of *never found by the army*? Or perhaps *never was and I am making this up*? Only wondering. Humans often use vague words to hide fearful truths.)

"So", and the G3 wife took a sip of her own coffee and smiled at Mrs. Shaw, "what brings you to Chicago, to this part of town? Are you looking for a long-term rental? Please tell me about yourself," and the words left her mouth and surrounded Mrs. Shaw's head, waiting. They had pursed lips and made peculiar side-long expressions as if they were ready to refute the expected answers.

Mrs. Shaw stirred her coffee (which she never drank) and placed both ringless hands in her lap as she stared into the face of the woman across from her. "I moved to Chicago about a month ago from a small town in southern Illinois. I needed to find a well-paying job, and I did, but my current hotel is costly and takes much of my available salary. I'm looking for a less expensive but safe place to live. I work down the street on Western at an office, and I am also starting work at the diner which is near you, the one on thirty-fifth street, and I need to be close to both. If you decide to rent to me, I will be able to walk to both places and save transportation money."

"That sounds reasonable," and the G3 wife took additional sips from her cup. "Why do you need two jobs, if I can ask? Couldn't you find work in your hometown?"

"I lived with my sister and her husband and," Mrs. Shaw cleared her throat (Throat clearing in humans, I have found, is a sure sign of some sort of insincerity, a stall for time, but judge for yourself.) "…and their little girl, my niece. The little girl is sickly, and money is needed for doctors and medicine. I could not earn enough there to help them with all the bills. I found a job here and am able to send them money a couple times a month. That's why I have the two jobs."

"What a good aunt! What a good sister! I am sure we can come to some sort of arrangement. Let me take you up to the rooms, and we can talk about rent and other issues."

The women went up my stairs, examined the rooms, had additional conversations, and an agreement was formed. A lease was signed. A week later, Ellen Shaw moved in. She had one medium suitcase, a cloth bag filled with various items, a coat she carried, and her purse. Not much. She came on a Monday evening, spending the night organizing the few things she brought with her. The next morning, she rose early, left for her job at the office, returned before dark. Monday through Friday, she worked at her office job. Wednesday, Thursday, and Friday evenings, and all Saturday, she worked her second job, at the diner. She was a creature of habit, and I learned her unvaried schedule which is included here:

Sunday: This was the only day she did not work. At first, she attended early church services. I know this because she asked the G3 wife where convenient churches were located. But after a time, she stayed in bed sleeping later, and only rarely ventured out to church. This was a busy day for her, and she always appeared tired. Arrangements had been made with the G3 wife to use the downstairs washing machine on Sundays, so the afternoon was spent cleaning, brushing, repairing, and ironing her clothes. Slowly, she added a few necessary items of clothing from the second-hand stores she visited. Sometimes when weather was decent, she would cross the boulevard to sit on a bench in the median, and although a book was in her hands, she generally spent the hours watching children as they played.

Monday: After returning from work and eating her evening meal (more about her meals later), she would take a bath and wash her hair, and while it dried, would sit at the table writing a letter, which she took with her the next day. I assume to mail it. I don't know what the letters said because, unlike Professor Uncle Henry, she did not read them aloud. However, once they were written and sealed, she would kiss the envelope and whisper, "I love and miss you, my darling girl." These words would lift up, swaying and moving in an adoring fashion, attaching themselves to each other in a soft and tender manner while finding a space to huddle together. The letters must have been sent to her sister because every other week, she would include a smaller envelope which contained carefully counted and folded money.

Tuesday: Ellen returned later on these days, after having done some grocery shopping. I noted the items she bought, and they rarely changed: a small loaf of bread, four thin slices of ham or bologna, four thin slices of cheese, a small jar of Peter Pan peanut butter and some Smucker's grape jelly (these last items only needed to be replaced every few weeks), Lipton tea bags (when needed), and three or four pieces of fruit, usually apples or bananas, although sometimes small plums or grapes or oranges appeared. Sometimes a package of sandwich cookies or fig newtons came out of the paper bags. Once there was a box of Girl Scout cookies, and during the early fall, a small cake appeared. That was the evening she placed the cake on the table and whispered to herself "Happy birthday to me!", cried for a time, the sobs melting into the woodwork (I really dislike wet emotions.), and then ate a large slice of the small cake. The groceries were stored in the Kelvinator next to a jar of mustard, a box of sugar cubes, and a container of pickles, all of which were periodically replaced. Tuesday's dinner was a sandwich. Additional sandwiches were made with the deli meat and cheese or the peanut butter, then wrapped in waxed paper and stored in the icebox as lunches and sometimes dinner for the week. Some Mondays, when the week's groceries had been eaten, she would come home from work carrying a small white bag which held a hot dog or a hamburger. This, with a cup of the Lipton tea, was dinner.

Wednesday, Thursday, Friday: Before leaving for her office job, Ellen would pack both her lunch and her black waitress uniform (purchased at the second-hand store) for her second job. She went to the diner right after the office and worked until it closed at nine. By nine-thirty on those nights, she was in bed, exhausted from her day. On Thursdays, she was in bed by ten, having taken her second bath of the week (she was allowed two). Some Friday evenings, she returned later because she was sometimes closed and locked the diner. Those evenings, she could barely drag herself up my stairs, and it was late when she was able to get to sleep.

Saturday: Ellen alternated working the early morning shift (7AM-4PM) or the later shift (2PM-10PM) at the diner. On those early morning days, she would stop at the corner drugstore after work, and on the late shift days, she would go before work. The drugstore (which was on the corner next to the diner) had two phone booths in the back. Ellen would enter one to make a phone call which lasted about ten minutes. How do I know this? The drugstore let the cinder alley know and therefore I knew. I also knew what went on in the diner because it told the drugstore who told the cinder alley who let me know. Few things done by humans remain secret.

This is how I am aware of Ellen's agreement with the diner's owner. When she asked about working there, she offered to work only for the tips if she could have regular meals and coffee there. The owner agreed. This is how she saved money and provided food for herself on the four nights she worked. Saturday nights, a bag containing diner leftovers became her Sunday meal, and sometimes there was enough for Monday's dinner. Ellen was conscientious with both her food and her money. She counted her tip money, placing the dimes, nickels, pennies in piles, adding them up, arranging them, and smiling when there was the occasional quarter. The tip money was divided into three uneven parts. Most of it was exchanged for paper bills, placed in an envelope along with other paper bills from her office salary, and sent in the letter to her sister. The next pile was used for grocery shopping and the few items bought from the second-hand store. A smaller pile was placed in a little container and shoved to the back of a dresser drawer. I wasn't sure what that money was meant for. At least not for a while.

Other than what the G3 wife had placed around as decoration in my rooms, the space remained unadorned except for one item. The first night Ellen came, she pulled from her suitcase a photograph in a frame. She stared at it for a long time, kissed it, and spoke the same words I became used to hearing after she wrote her weekly letters.

"I love and miss you, my darling girl," she said, and then placed the framed photo on the table next to the bed.

Sometimes, especially when she was writing those letters, she would take the framed photo and move it to the table where she would look at it as she wrote. Other times she put it on the dresser. *What a great aunt*, were the words spoken by the G3 wife and at first, I just accepted that notion. However, after a time, I considered what the relationship could actually be. Humans lie at times, out of necessity, fearful of what society would do if they were honest, if the harsh truth were known. You see, there were two people in the photo: Ellen and a very thin, very young girl. Ellen's arm was around the child and they were looking at each other and smiling, and the little girl looked exactly like Ellen. Same eyes and chin and hair coloring even though the photo was black and white. Same smile. Same identical teeth. Same. Very much so. Of course, if this was her niece, there would be a family resemblance. I never saw a photograph of the child's supposed parents, but thought to myself: *Hmm. Hmm.*

One Saturday afternoon, shortly after Ellen had moved in, she came home from the early shift, and before going up the stairs, walked to the kitchen where the G3 wife was cleaning and cutting vegetables. She stood for a moment. The wife saw her and smiled and the following conversation took place:

"Oh hello, dear, is there something I can do for you?"

"Actually, there is. I have a small favor to ask," and as Ellen spoke, her words left her lips and became both shaky and weepy, although Ellen's face remained stoic. "My niece is not doing well. She had been in the hospital for a few days but is now home. I call my sister each week from the phones at the drugstore, but there was no way for her to get in touch with me when this happened. I was wondering if I may give my sister your telephone number just in case something happens which I should know about. She would not call your telephone except for a real emergency," and these words joined the others, all of them quivery and quaky.

"Oh, Mrs. Shaw, I am so sorry to hear that. Of course you should give your sister my number. I do hope she never needs to use it, but if it will make you feel more comfortable, then please do that," and the G3 wife wiped her hands on a towel. She was unable to note what I could: that Ellen's words, once hearing this, let out a relieved sigh and floated to the ceiling, becoming straighter and steadier as they melted together.

Ellen thanked the wife and returned to her room.

Ellen Shaw. I will admit that I am having trouble explaining her. She was alone in the room, rarely speaking to herself, unlike Professor

Uncle Henry; not reading letters and examining photographs and talking to a companion as Robert Richardson did; hardly practicing thievery and arguing like the Hodgkins family, and so, I can only guess at her potential secrets, her likely insincerity, her possible lies. Her harsh and hidden truth. Was there a fear of censure from society? Was there a veiled reason she left the small town? I'm not one to judge, but I began to have certain suspicions. She was truly solitary. During the months she stayed, she never, not even once, had a friend or companion who visited. She may not have made any friends. Except for the few times she would cross the boulevard to sit on a bench in the median, or the rare Sundays she would attend church, she did not leave except for work. And work, she did. Worked and slept and cleaned and followed her schedule without fail. Oh, there were a few times she cried, but they were not loud sobbing tears, and she soon stopped or fell asleep. She kissed the letters and the photograph she had on display uttering the same words: *I love you and miss you, my darling girl,* but except for that, she was mostly quiet. A few tears. A few words. I started to worry about the sturdiness, the hardiness, the mightiness of my walls, my woodwork and windows and bricks upstairs, but there was nothing to do. I simply watched and considered and was grateful that she did not pry up baseboards to hide liquor bottles or damage any of the windows by leaning out too far, or allow forbidden cigarette smoke to cloud my walls like so many of the men boarders had done. Ellen Shaw, *Mrs. Charles Shaw,* avoided fuss and frays and frenzy, and for that I was grateful. But there was something, something I did not understand about her. There was an unrevealed part to her. Insincerity? Lies? Perhaps. You can judge. I don't.

Ellen continued to divide her tip money, placing the smallest amount into the container in her drawer until it was almost full. Then, one evening in autumn, as the weather was getting colder and windier and snow would arrive soon, she took out the container and spread the money on the table. She divided the coins into piles: pennies, nickels, dimes, a few quarters, counted it, and placed the coins into a wallet she kept in her purse. She ate a sandwich (being a Monday night) took a bath, washed her hair, and wrote her weekly letter before going to bed. The following night, she returned later than usual, holding her bag of groceries and another, smaller bag. Groceries were put away, dinner sandwich eaten, preparations for weekly lunches completed, and only then did she place the smaller bag on the table and remove the contents. Had I not been familiar with children's toys, I would not have known what this item was. I did. It was a box containing a doll. The box had some see-through material covering it with words on the front, and it was possible to see the doll inside which looked like a human baby. But it wasn't. Just a toy. As Ellen examined the box, she ran her hands over the thing and quietly read the words which were printed on it. I was surprised at her voice, but pleased that the words which floated up to the highest point in the corner walls, cuddled together in playfulness.

"Ideal Toy Company presents Betsy-Wetsy. Includes feeding bottle and extra diaper. Additional layette sold separately. Eyes with lashes. Jointed arms and legs. Ten inches of a soft vinyl body. Oh, my darling girl, I wish I could see your face when you open this at Christmas! It was worth the eight dollars!" and Ellen sat and held the box containing the toy for quite a while. Then she picked up the photo, kissed it again and spoke the usual words.

The box was placed back into the bag and set on the table. However, the next few nights, she moved the bag from place to place, I assume trying to find a hiding spot for it. Or a safe place, or just a place where it would be away from questioning eyes. Just in case. She put it under the bed, and then on top of the Kelvinator, then against the book case shelf, and even placed it inside her small suitcase, where it took up much of the space. I don't know what she was attempting to do, but when she opened the hall linen closet to pull out a towel, she looked up and said, "There!"

She dragged a chair from the table to the closet, and standing on it while holding the bag with the doll, she put it on the top-most shelf, towards the back. She was not satisfied, so she removed the boxed toy from the bag and placed the box itself towards the back where it just fit. She climbed down from the chair and looked up and whispered, "Perfect. It can't be seen. It will be safe there until I have the money to send it," and she replaced the chair, folded up the bag, and readied herself for bed. Humans. Why you do the things you do, I cannot fathom. Anyway, there it was, the small thin box containing a toy doll, and until today, there it remains. There is a bit more. Further explanation will come.

The weeks passed. The holiday called *Thanksgiving* came, and the G3 family joined together for the day. The best thing about it was that the noise and talk was often and loud, and I saw all the words and sounds climbing the air, latching onto each other, pushing into the spaces of the woodwork and walls and into the outer bricks, strengthening and filling whatever room there was, holding straight and hardy, and I was glad. The worst thing were the humans who made the noises. Especially the young ones. So difficult to withstand their yelling and fighting sounds and at the same time, so grateful for the yelling and fighting sounds. The G3 wife had invited Ellen Shaw to share dinner with the family, and, surprisingly, she accepted. On the Tuesday before the feast day, her grocery shopping included a greenish box with the words: *Marshall Field and Company Frango Mints* spread across it. As she took it out, she turned it over and around, speaking rare words aloud. "You better be worth the $1.65 I spent on you!" On Thanksgiving, she brought the box with her as she entered the kitchen, thanking the G3 wife for inviting her and handing her the candy. She was quiet at dinner, speaking rarely, eating lightly, and leaving the family after helping them clean up. She explained she was tired and was working all the following day at the diner because her office was closed. She took her usual Thursday night bath, went to bed, and cried for a time before falling asleep. One week later, the phone call came.

It was the following Thursday night and Ellen had just returned from working at the diner. There was no snow on the ground, but it was there, hanging in the outside air, waiting for lowered degrees to give it permission to drop. Ellen was going up the stairs when the G3 wife came out from the kitchen where she had been making her husband a cup of tea. She called out to Ellen who stopped with one foot on the floor and another on the first step.

"Mrs. Shaw, about an hour ago, there was a phone call for you, and it was your sister. She apologized for calling so late, but she said it was very important and asked you to get in touch right away. I said I would let you know, and I am. She sounded quite upset. To be honest, I believe she had been crying."

Ellen took a deep breath and her face lost some color.

"She didn't say what it was about?"

"No. Just that you needed to get in touch as soon as possible."

Ellen took her foot off the step and turned toward the woman. Her hand remained on the railing, and I waited to see if she would do the thing humans call "fainting" because it seemed she might. Instead, she said, "The corner drugstore is closed now, and I can't use their pay phones. Please allow me to call my sister from your telephone. I'll pay the cost of the call."

The G3 wife looked down at the cup she held, then nodded as she said, "Yes, as long as the call is short and you pay the cost, go ahead and call your sister. I can make you a cup of tea if you would like one."

"No, thank you. I'll make the call now," and Ellen placed her purse and bag next to the stairs as she walked to the telephone. The G3 wife waited a few seconds, and then went into the bedroom where her husband waited for his tea. Ellen used the telephone, and I heard the short conversation, but there were few words coming from Ellen who mostly listened. The words she did speak rose from her mouth in an agitated and anxious manner, distractedly pressing and thrusting against each other, squeezing into the ceiling and wall while frantic sighs fell down around Ellen's head. When the brief phone call was done, she sat in the chair, placed her head in her hands and was totally still. When she did get up, her ashen face had turned ghostly white.

The bedroom door, behind which I am sure the G3 wife was pressed against listening, opened, and she stepped out. "Mrs. Shaw, is there anything I can help with? I hope the news is not too bad."

Ellen looked at the wife and then, with shaky words, words which trembled and tottered all the way to the nearest wall, said, "My niece is very ill. She is in the hospital again and has been there for all this week. She is awfully sick, and I need to go home right now. I am sorry, but I need to pack and leave immediately. I don't know when or if I will be back, but I will call and let you know. I'm not sure when a train leaves from the downtown station, but I'm going there and will wait for one. Thanks, but there is nothing you can do," and she walked rapidly to the stairs.

"What about your jobs? Not sure a train will leave tonight, and it is rather late. Why don't you wait until morning and try to get some sleep? It will be easier traveling then because it's late and dark and cold now."

Ellen picked up her purse and bag and as she hurried up the stairs said, "I'll call the office and the diner as soon as I can, but I can't wait. I'll call for a taxi cab to pick me up in a half hour, if you don't mind me using the telephone again."

"Well, I can call for one if you want me to."

Ellen yelled back down the stairs, "Thank you, that would be helpful," and she entered the upstairs room as the G3 wife went to make the call.

As Ellen hurried upstairs, the words they spoke flew back and forth, between each other, overlapping and rushing, speeding to the ceiling and bumping against each other and the air until they found a spot near the ceiling's center to enter. The wife yelled up the stairs that a taxi would come in thirty minutes, and Ellen yelled back, "Thanks!"

and I watched as she sped around the rooms, grabbing and opening her suitcase, stuffing clothes into it, not folding anything, mixing dirty and clean clothing together. She shoved her few possessions into that suitcase, into her cloth bag, and rushed to the bathroom to grab her toothpaste and the few jars kept there. Luckily, she had a minimum of items to pack because there was a loud honking of a car horn outside just as she completed her hurried tasks. She turned off the lights and went down the stairs where the G3 wife and husband were standing in their bathrobes, waiting by my front door, switching the porch light on, lighting the darkness.

"Be careful, Mrs. Shaw. It's so late, and I'm worried about you being in that large train station by yourself. Are you sure you should leave now?"

Ellen answered her, "I'll be fine, and yes, I need to get home quickly. I'm sorry to go like this, but as soon as I know something, I'll call you. Thank you both," and she rushed down the porch steps into the waiting cab. She was gone.

I don't have connections as far as the downtown train station, so I have no idea whether she left that night or waited until morning, if she sat alone in that place or found a coffee shop open and spoke to someone, if she cried while she waited or sat still, looking straight ahead, worrying. There is nothing else I can tell you about that evening, about her journey, about her concerns, but the remainder of the week and through the weekend, the G3 wife blabbered constantly about the situation. I admit, I was glad for her many words which continually rose up, flapping and bustling and shrugging. They pushed into the walls, into the wood, into the outer bricks. She ran to the telephone each time it rang, saying, "I'll bet that's Mrs. Shaw calling. I wonder what has happened?" But there was no word from her for many days, until one morning, as the wife was dusting the front parlor furniture, the telephone rang. It startled her, and she let out a shrill *yip* which rushed to the closed window, knocking itself on the floor. As the wife went to the phone, the *yip* picked itself up, looked around to see if any words or sounds were watching (And, yes, a number of them stared down from the window's woodwork, making giggling faces and pointing motions.) and floated to the side wall as if nothing had happened. Words and sounds sometimes act just like the humans who make them.

The wife answered the call and sat in the chair as she listened. I could not hear the other person, but gathered it was Ellen Shaw, and I filled in the conversation and determined the meaning based on the words the wife spoke. I'm sure you can too:

"I am glad to hear from you…"

"Oh no, I am SO sorry. What a terrible thing to happen…"

"Were you able to be with her when…?"

"Well, I understand. You need to stay there and…"

"The things left here, do you want me to…"

"Fine. I'll do that. Again, I'm so sorry for your loss. I will say a prayer for that little angel. Please don't hesitate to let me know how you're doing, and I'll take care of the things…"

"Yes. Well, OK. I will. Good-by, Mrs. Shaw…"

Conversation over. Telephone hung up. The wife sat in the chair and sighed and spoke out loud, "Poor woman and poor parents. Such a terrible thing to happen. I suppose I need to get upstairs and take care of things. So sad. So sad."

That is what I know. The wife finished her dusting, then walked up the stairs to the now vacant rooms. She spoke aloud to the walls and herself, and that conversation I can report.

She looked around the two rooms remarking, "Well, there is some clean-up to be done, but Mrs. Shaw was certainly not as messy as those men. I should get a bag or box and bring it up to put the things in. First, I need to clean out the Kelvinator. Leaving any foodstuffs up here will be a mistake," and she opened the refrigerator door to peer in.

"Hmm, not much here. I'll take what I can carry down and decide if it is worth keeping or not," and she took out the two wrapped sandwiches, the couple slices of bread left, and an apple. Then she closed the door and went to her kitchen. Nothing else was taken from the upstairs rooms that day.

The following day, she climbed the stairs bringing bags and a box with her. The remaining foods were removed from the refrigerator and a bookcase shelf. She cleaned out the Kelvinator and wiped it down, All the drawers and closed areas were examined, and a few items of mostly second-hand store clothing were placed into the box. There was only a used bar of soap left in the bathroom, and when the medicine cabinet was opened, a partial container of aspirin was removed. The only thing in the bedroom was a sweater which sported missing buttons, and the waitress uniform which Ellen didn't bother packing. There must not have been a need for it in Ellen Shaw's small home town. Just as the G3 wife was leaving, she spied the photo of Ellen and the small girl. It had fallen back against the wall on the dresser. She held the photo in both hands, examining it.

"Oh, this must be that poor little girl. How pretty she is, or was, and she looks so much like her auntie. Mrs. Shaw must have forgotten this. She said to dispose of anything she left, but I'll keep this downstairs just in case I hear from her, and she wants it back as a remembrance. Such a shame. So sad." And the wife took the framed photograph with her, placing it on a table in the parlor with framed photos of the G3 family.

Over the following days, the rooms were cleaned, dusted, and made ready for a new occupant. However, there was no advertising placard placed into the window, facing outward where it could be viewed and read. The rooms remained empty for some months. Not because the money wasn't wanted or needed. It was. Not because there was a sweet memory of Ellen Shaw. There wasn't. But, as the G3 wife said to the G3 husband, "I am not sure I want to have any more messy men as boarders just now. Let's hold off for a time. I would just like to have the rooms empty for a bit. Is that OK?"

It was. They were. And the months passed. Eventually, the placard was placed properly, the rooms were once again rented, this time, to a somewhat fussy, fastidious man who kept the rooms almost as clean as Ellen Shaw had. The G3 wife was satisfied, and he stayed for a long time, never causing a problem, keeping to himself, continuing to be politely aloof. I can hear you asking, what about the hidden doll in the upstairs linen closet, in the corner on the upper shelf? It remains. More to tell. And Ellen Shaw was never heard from again.

Before the fussy newcomer moved in, the G3 wife worked at cleaning and organizing her kitchen. In one of the kitchen cabinets, there were several large platters, an old teapot, some small figurines which had a few chips, and a variety of unused towels and tablecloths which had what humans call "sentimental value". The wife wanted to keep them, but needed the cabinet space, so it was all packed into two boxes. The husband was given the task to *store them in the upstairs linen closet, on the high shelf, pushed to the side where they will be out of the way.* He did. And when he shoved them back and out of the way, muttering,

"Junk! Just get rid of this stuff! No need to store it or keep it!", those words, along with an aggravated nudge from the husband, managed to angrily shove and push the Betsy-Wetsy box back into the uppermost corner, grinding into the space, opening the small crack found there just enough so that the entire toy box (which was not that large) was jammed into it. It could not be seen from below. The husband never bothered to investigate the slight noise the box made as it fell into the expanded corner, because the baseball game was on, and he was annoyed at missing part of it while having to complete the task. "There, done," he grumbled. "Stupid junk!"

The doll in the box is still there. I'm unsure why Ellen did not take it with her when she left. Perhaps she forgot about it. Maybe there was no time to pull out a chair and stand on it and retrieve it. Possibly she thought she would be back at some point. Whatever the case, the doll in the box remains. No thin little girl held the soft ten-inch vinyl body while humming a lullaby and play-feeding it the bottle and changing the wet diaper for the extra dry one which was included. No moving the jointed arms and legs and pretending a real baby was moving and wiggling. No brushing small real hands against tiny fake eyelashes attached to painted blue eyes. No pennies saved to purchase the extra baby layette which was sold separately. No cuddles were given as a small sick girl held the doll closely at night, sinking into a restless sleep, arms tucked around the toy, dreams of a happy and healthy life rolling through her mind. Did I make you sad just now? Well, stop it. Human life goes on.

Can you stand more unhappy human news? Here it comes. A year or so after Ellen Shaw left and just after the fussy new boarder moved in, the G3 husband dropped dead. He was walking in my backyard, looking up at the tree when he gave a loud, long gasp (It shot up into the underside of the gutter, hung there for a long time and eventually disappeared.), put his hand to his chest, and fell so hard into the ground that something on his left side cracked. Broken bones on a dead person don't need to be fixed, as I understand it. Anyway, with the husband gone, the G3 wife began to act strangely. Sometimes she would forget to dress until it was night, and then, as the sky darkened, she would put on a clean outfit and wear it to bed. The laundry didn't get done. She sometimes wore the same clothes for a week, until her daughter-in-law showed up and made her bathe and change clothes. The wife would forget to eat. And one time she ate an entire jar of pickles, vomiting them in the middle of the night. Disgusting noises pushed into the bathroom wall just above the sink. She would forget to collect rent from the fussy boarder or the downstairs boring couple, but the money would be handed to her (such honesty!) and she would place it in one of the drawers in the kitchen, forgetting about it. Her bills went unpaid; the ice trays weren't filled; and there was no sweet lemonade to serve when the grandchildren came over. She would forget the sugar. She made cookies but either forgot to bake them or to take them from the oven. Once someone called the fire department when smoke was seen billowing out of the open kitchen window. She was unsure of who was who when the neighbor women visited, and when asked about the photos displayed on the parlor table, she wasn't clear about who they were. Finally, it was decided by her son and daughter-in-law that she could no longer live alone. The grandchildren were grown and on their own by this time, so the son and his wife sold their own house and moved back to me, allowing the G3 wife to live out her life with family around. Arrangements were made, moving trucks were called, lawyers gave counsel, and the couple moved in to take care of me. And the G3 wife. I knew these people however, so for me the transition was easy. The son and his wife settled in.

The G3 wife lived in her own created world, not quite knowing where she was, who she was, or who the others around her were. She would wander through me, looking around as if she had never seen my once familiar walls and windows, doors and stairs. Daily, she would examine all the photos on the tables, giving them names and lives and relationships she created, not remembering who they actually were. She would pick them up and speak to them, and her words would rise from her lips, look around, unsure of where they were supposed to go, uncertain of their task, unclear about who the surrounding words were. Eventually, some older words from the ceiling and walls, some stronger emotions from the floors and windows, would appear and gently guide the new words into a space where they huddled together looking insecure and unconvinced. The G3 wife held the photo of her mother and said "Oh yes, cousin so-and-so, I remember the fun we had on your farm." Gazing at the wedding photo of her son and his wife, she giggled and claimed, "There I am with my husband. Don't I look happy!" And when the photo of Ellen Shaw and the little girl she asserted was her niece was examined, the wife nodded and said, "Ah, there I am with my daughter. I think she lives here with me. I will go and find her and ask her about this photo." But when she turned to look for the daughter she never had, she forgot the task and placed the photo in the kitchen refrigerator.

On an early evening, after a difficult day's work, the son came home, went to the kitchen and reached into the refrigerator for a bottle of beer. He pushed aside a plate and saw the photo which he removed. Staring and smiling at each other in black and white stillness was Ellen Shaw and the now dead little girl she called her niece. The son held the photo as he examined it, but did not recognize the woman or the girl, and knew that asking his mother who they were would be useless. He said to his wife, "These must be some relatives, but I don't know them. Oh well!" I watched him place the photograph of Ellen and the little girl back with the others, putting it between one of his dead father who was laughing and pointing at something in my backyard and another of his long-dead grandmother holding a small child. The people in those photographs, he recognized. When eventually the house was sold and all the framed photos were packed into a box, Ellen and her niece took their place with the G3 family, their relatives and friends. All of them placed against each other in the box, snug and sheltered and safe.

13

The Alley

Red calls me *the cinder alley,* in an attempt to annoy me even though he is aware that I have been a PAVED ALLEY for almost two decades. I ignore him. After all, I am much older, having been around practically from the start of the city. None of us alleys even had cinders then. We were muddy paths, and I am not ashamed to admit that. At our start, some alleys towards the center of the city had wooden blocks placed on top of their mud. Eventually, cinders were shoveled on the rest of us, and finally, after decades, as the city continued to expand and improve, many of us were paved, although for some, asphalt was used. I am part of a community within a community. You see, the alleys in Chicago are more extensive than any other such areas in the entire country. Placed together, we would cover 1,900 miles. So, mud or blocks or asphalt or paved, we travel through the various areas, both separating and connecting the streets and houses, the blocks and medians, the play areas and repair shops and garages, and have done so since the 1830's, when the original plat for the City of Chicago was drawn up. We were part of the planning. We are not mistakes.

Red and I tolerate each other. I have better relationships with other houses on the block, and am actually quite friendly with many of the garages. That is probably due to the fact that my pavement attaches to their bases. Closeness necessitates friendship. At least in our cases. I think one of the reasons I have been allowed this space in the book is because of information which, over the years, I have shared with Red. Because of my length, I have the ability to communicate with many of the places he cannot, and most of what I learn from the corner drugstore and even the bit I know from thirty-fifth street (my pavement butts against that street's pavement in one area), I share with Red. Perhaps this is his attempt to make up for the things he has said about me. Whatever the case, the truth is, I have not told him everything. There are some conversations only I have been privy to, some things even he does not know, although after these few pages are written I suppose he will. So will you.

I have seen my share of human behavior over the decades. Much of it grim, some of it dreadful, a portion of it mischievous, a snippet of it immature, all of it awkward. I do not have a head to turn away or eyes and ears to close, and it is all there for me to bear it witness. The muggings, the sorrows, the conversations, the pointless displays of anger or blustering or even romance. Yes, I have seen it all. Even, and it was many long decades ago, when I was still a muddy pathway, a murder. But I will not bore you with the recitation of these many human activities because only a very few have to do with the people who lived in Red. The ones you, as a reader, will know. For example, there was the son in what has been labeled the "G1 family".

The son in that family was upset when his mother remarried. The yelling and fighting from the kitchen could be easily heard throughout the yard and into my space. The son often smashed his way out of the back door, storming onto my cinder path, walking angrily, talking loudly, even swearing periodically as he stumped up one way and down another. This happened before the garage was built, when there was a small picket fence between the yard and me, and that fence took the brunt of the son's anger. Once the G2 husband moved in and decided to build the garage, it took just a few jerks and pushes to have that fence tumble down upon both me and the yard. It was weakened due to the son having so often kicked it in fury and frustration. Actually, I was surprised it had remained standing, and during some violent and heavy rain or snow storms, I was positive it would collapse. But it endured. Quiveringly and totteringly, it remained. The last and greatest argument between the son and the stepfather was when the boy stalked out and did not return for the entire night. I understand that the following morning, he told his mother he had spent the night at a friend's house. He did not. He raged out of the house, stalked up my path and was gone until dark. His mother, the G1 wife, continually peeked out from the kitchen window in the back. I assume she also did the same in the front of the house, but there was no sign of the son. Of course there was not. He was hiding two garages down, propped up against the back of the garage where he could not be seen. He was not at a friend's place, but spent that night, his jacket pulled up around his neck, his cap pulled down over his face, hunched in the corner, periodically kicking against my cinders, sometimes crying. I witnessed it all. In the morning when the sun woke him from what was surely an uncomfortable sleep, he got up, shook out his clothing, and urinated against the neighbor's fence. Unpleasant, but I have seen worse. Don't ask. He raked his fingers through his hair, placed his cap on, and walked to the end of me before turning right onto one sidewalk and then right onto the one leading to his house. I assumed he wanted to enter the front door, giving no hint as to where he spent the night. Red told me that he left the house soon after, moving into an apartment with someone. Probably for the best.

Housemaid #2 often stood in my cinders with the other housemaids, talking, laughing, consoling each other as personal problems were discussed. They complained about or poked fun at the families they worked for and their problems. Sometimes one of them had a cigarette snitched from her employer's stash, and they shared it, each taking a puff, passing it around until it was gone, throwing the burned-out butt end into my cinders. After a party for which they had cleaned and cooked, baked and served, and cleaned again, leftover cake would be shared, each woman taking a small piece. They were a close group of women, and when one brought the news about the offer of a better job in a ritzier neighborhood, or the exciting news of an engagement to a long-time beau, hugs and congratulations were given, and nothing negative was said. At least until the next time the lucky woman was absent from the group. Then her luck was discussed using words which were hardly, umm, cordial. Housemaid #2 was one of the most vocal women in this group, and when Robert Richardson moved into the house, she was filled with exciting news about him. She was quite taken with the man.

"He has the most lovely hair and is very sweet looking," and the other women nodded and passed around the stolen cigarette as she spoke. "I put an extra pat of butter in his oats this morning, and he told me the oats were delicious. *Delicious* was the word he used," and she took her turn at the almost burnt-out cigarette.

"But," and the housemaid who had brought the smoking treat for everyone, suggested, "he might have a sweetheart somewhere. He could be in a relationship. You don't know that yet, do you?"

"No," and housemaid #2 shrugged her shoulder as if the question had landed on it like a fly, "but I am sure he watched me as I walked back to the kitchen,"

"Probably wiggling a bit," said another, and all the housemaids laughed. Even housemaid #2 smirked as she walked in imitation of her earlier sashay.

For a time, she would mention to the others the small services she completed for Robert Richardson: two clean towels a week rather than just one, extra oats in his morning bowl, shiny boots which she had wiped clean. She explained that she was sure he had *smiled meaningfully at me,* had *thanked me greatly,* and she expected a *friendship to turn to something more,* and at the last comment the housemaids glanced at each other, eyes lowered but slight, knowing smiles wreathing their lips. They did not believe that would happen, and once when housemaid #2 was not in attendance, their discussion centered on the doubtful romance, the sad state of housemaid #2's unrequited love, her obvious misunderstanding of Robert Richardson's true nature. His *true nature* was expounded upon by one of the housemaids who told the others she had watched as Richardson and some male friend of his sat on a bench in the median, hands touching at times, smiling at each other, moving closer until their shoulders met. "Ah, the girl is in for a shock. She does not understand what I do," and the gossiping housemaid shook her head. I'm unsure the others understood what was being suggested, but they went along with the story because the woman telling the gossip was older and obviously wiser in the ways of the world.

After a time, housemaid #2 stopped mentioning Richardson, shrugged when asked about him, shook off the possibility of a budding romance, and, in time, after his death was announced, began to speak of the new beau, this time an actual one: the butcher at a nearby shop. She did not seem as enthused about this one. And when, one by one, the housemaids left their positions because the economic situation their employers found themselves in did not allow for hired help, housemaid #2 stood in my cinders by herself. She was the last to leave, and that day, she leaned against the garage which butted up against my cinders, tears running down her cheeks, eyes staring into the sky, hands rubbing over her belly which had a small protrusion. I'm unsure what happened to her and her butcher husband, but she did not appear to be happy. I have noted that humans rarely are.

Then there was Junior. Housemaid #2 spent many hours standing on my cinders, and Junior spent almost as much time. Usually, he was hiding from his parents. He would leave the house in the morning, move down the sidewalk towards the school and make a quick turn onto my cinders where he would skulk along the garages, peeking through the yards, hiding until later in the morning when he would travel through some of the 1900 miles of my companion alleys, looking for personal effects. Others' personal effects. He brought the items back, stood behind the garage, talking to himself, examining the man's shirt he took from a clothesline or a toy he gathered from a yard. If these things passed his inspection, he would take them somewhere and exchange them for a few pennies. He whispered to himself as he stood hiding and counting his coins.

"Let me see," he would mumble, "if I give the old man three pennies, I can keep two for myself," and he would place two coins in his pocket before changing his mind. "No, I better give four and keep one. Next time I'll keep three," and he rubbed the side of his face which displayed a fading yellow-greenish bruise. "Better hide this coin first. Pockets being checked by the dirty bloke all the time now. Nasty coot!" He would wait until late afternoon to go into the house. Sometimes I heard shouting from the upper floor although I was never sure who was doing the yelling or what was being said.

Usually late at night, Junior would sneak out of the house and hide behind the garage. At times, he would spit some blood into my cinders or rub his stomach or ears. Then he would place his face into his arms and ugly sobs would come from the boy. "I hate them! I hate them both," he would whine, wiping blood onto his already dirty sleeve. "Just wait until I got my cash. I'll do something to them before I go! I'll let them know how I hate their guts!" He would stay like this for the night and then slink back in the house. These times became more frequent, and I watched as he kept more of the coins he collected, whispering to himself the new amounts the nickel or pennies would add to his hidden stash. At times, he would drone on about his plans, about where he might go when he left, about the new name he would give himself. It was this last item which he seemed to enjoy mulling about. "Gonna change the stupid last name too," he would grumble, "Maybe *Jones* or *Wilson*, something fine." He would practice his possible names. "*Michael Wilson* or *Jonathan Jones*. Maybe *Harold* and tell people I am *Hank. Hank.* Great name. Sounds tough!" And he would practice the possibilities saying: "Hello. I'm George Johnson. Call me George," or "My name is Edward Robins, but friends call me Ned. Glad to meet ya!" Names would change, but with each one Junior would shake his head saying "No, not that one." This activity was at least less disgusting than his spitting on my cinders after a smack across his face, or vomiting into the weeds growing along the garage after a kick to his stomach. Had I been able to feel charity, I might have for him. Over the decades, I have viewed too much of people's inhumanity to each other, and in this regard, I agree with Red: humans are loathsome.

Finally, the expected nasty clash happened, and the entire Hodgkins group was expelled into the street. I didn't need Red to tell me this news. It was clearly heard throughout the block, neighbors speaking of it for weeks over back fences and while walking from their garages. But Red was not the only one who was aware of the Hodgkins group sneaking back into the yard that night, their stay under the back stairs, the revenge Junior enacted upon his sleeping parents. I heard it all. Whispering carries through night air. What I do know that Red does not, at least not until now, is the final name Junior Hodgkins christened himself as he left. After the pilfering of Sam's money, the exchange of hats, the token of disgust and anger displayed by Junior's fingers as he snuck from the yard, he whispered his thoughts. He talked to himself saying, "There, you four-flushers. Both of youse. Won't make me the fall guy now. I'm goin' places. Have *your* stash. Got me a new ritzy hat. And a new name…" and by this point, Junior was at the area where I connected with thirty-fifth street. He stopped. He glanced one way and then another. He nodded, and in the darkness, I could hear his smile as he turned right and spoke in a perfectly normal voice, "And here I come: Ralph Fisher. CALL ME ROCCO!" The newly named Ralph Rocco Fisher began to run through the night streets yelling his name: "ROCCO! ROCCO! ROCCO!" until it faded into a soft sound, becoming an incomprehensible babble, then a low drone, and finally, silence. While I'm unsure exactly what happened to Rocco, I heard rumors about his connections with some south side gang, a Chicago mob. Who knows if it's true? Stranger things have happened.

There were boarders in the house who used me as a walkway, as a shortcut, and I heard their secrets, their stories, but the boarder who spent the most time in me was Uncle Henry. Once he began to work on the garden, he discovered that resting on the old chair placed against the garage was a comfortable spot to take a break. He often spoke out loud, probably just to hear his own voice, and when he became friendly with the neighbor whose house was on the other side of me, he was delighted. There was someone to listen. As he was plotting out the garden, turning over the dirt, readying it for the plants, he took a break and glanced down my cinder path. "Well," he declared to himself, "there's a chair. Perfect for a short rest," and he opened the back gate, moved the chair against the garage and lowered himself on to it. "Ah, yes," and he settled in, his back to the chair's back, "this is excellent." Over the next few days, after gardening, he moved the chair, sat in it, and smiled, watching the sky, commenting to himself about the clouds and the wind or lack of either, and appeared content. One day, he pulled some papers out from his pocket and looked through them, reading parts aloud. He hadn't read much when the neighbor from the other house came out through his yard with a bag of trash and heard his voice.

"What is that?" he called, "Are you talking to me?"

Uncle Henry looked up from the papers and smiled. "No, I was just rereading this old letter, but I would be happy to talk with you if you have the time,"

The neighbor threw the trash into the container and turned to him. "I certainly have the time. Nothing but time left for this old man," and he went into his yard where he grabbed a rickety wooden chair and brought it with him. "Mind if I set this down and talk?"

"Delighted!" and Uncle Henry, coughing a bit, moved over to make room for the neighbor, and they began what would become a running conversation about the weather, the garden, the high price of new shoes and clothes, the lack of politeness from young people, the state of the city, the country, the world, and eventually a bit about themselves. Through the months, they shared personal information, and it was in this way I learned about Mrs. Marjorie Andrews, the woman who should have received Uncle Henry's fifty-dollars.

She and Uncle Henry had grown up together and were friends. They shared some flirtations, went to their high school senior picnic together, and, as Uncle Henry, after a short coughing spell, explained to the neighbor, "I would have asked Margie if she thought we had a future together, but I was shy in those days, and was going away to college, and when I came back, she had gone and married someone else. I had just myself to blame, because we had kept up a correspondence, but I was afraid to mention a future together in a letter. I thought I could do it better when I was with her, but," and he sighed heartily at this point and coughed into his handkerchief, "I kept putting it off until it was too late."

The neighbor nodded. "Well, hindsight, I suppose. I married my wife when we were both just nineteen. Been together all these years, and it was the best thing I ever did. Did you ever find another woman?"

Uncle Henry shook his head while clearing his throat. "No. Margie and I continued a correspondence for years, and I even visited her and the husband a couple times. He was a decent man, and they seemed happy. Had two daughters and a few grandkids. I always wondered how things might have been if I hadn't been so closed-mouth. Once I found out that her husband died, I wasted time again. Wanted to give her time to grieve, but then some widow at her church came along, and she married him. That's what I do. Take too much time to think and not act," and he turned his head to cough again.

"Lesson learned, I guess," and the neighbor grimaced in appreciation of Uncle Henry's lost chances and constant coughing. "Don't wait too long to make those important decisions. Right?"

"Absolutely. I've written to her a few times in the past few years, but haven't heard back. Letters weren't returned, and I think I would have heard if something happened to her. Last address I have is in Kansas City, Missouri. Not sure if it's the correct one. Is that your wife waving to you?"

The neighbor looked over to his wife standing on the back steps. "Yep. That's her. Ball and chain. I better get going. She needed light bulbs changed or something. Take care now, and watch that cough." He dragged the old chair back to his yard and disappeared into the house.

Uncle Henry watched him leave and sat back and cleared his throat once more. He coughed and sighed and nodded as he spoke to himself. "You are correct, old friend, I won't wait long to make important decisions. Not long at all. In fact, I know what this last important decision will be." Another coughing fit happened, and when he was able to stand up, he moved the chair out of the way, wrapped the scarf he always wore around his neck and went back to his garden. Fall was approaching. Uncle Henry checked the garden mums which were just beginning to flower, and he bent towards them. "Lovely," I heard him comment, "so glad I am still here for a while to appreciate you, my flowered friends." He stood up, swaying and coughing, and then, wrapping his scarf around his neck once again, went into the house. Uncle Henry was gone for good soon after that. I don't know what happened with the woman he talked about. Sometimes mysteries remain mysteries.

Different humans moved in and out of Red. Some lived upstairs, others lived in the garden apartment, and one couple who lived in the garden apartment, the Taylors, Carolyn and Patrick, used to…

Wait a minute…

Excuse me…………………………………………………………………

…………………………………………………………………………………

Sorry, that was Red. I have been told to stop. He said the Taylor's story has not yet been told, and the secret is his to explain, so I will end this. Frankly, I am surprised Red has allowed me to continue, and I wish I could tell the story I know about…………………………………………

OK……………………….. I'm finished. Have to go.

14

Back to Me

I warned the cinder alley (Yes, I know: *paved*.) not to overstep my book boundaries. He knew the story of the Taylors hasn't yet been explained because it's part of *my* history. You will learn about it, but first, back to ME and the human changes in *my* space.

So, the G3 wife. She went the way of all humans. She wandered around my rooms, getting lost in the once familiar spaces, roaming outside and down the streets, searching for someone she thought she needed to see. When her son and daughter-in-law missed her, they would look for her and bring her back to me. But once, they were both out, leaving the G3 wife alone, and when they did return, it was too late. She had left my porch, had wandered into the street, had gotten herself hit by a truck traveling down the boulevard, turning onto thirty-fifth street, the driver unable to see the old woman who did not bother to watch at the corner because she forgot about the traffic, the hurrying cars, the mammoth-sized trucks. The corner drugstore noted it and passed the info to the cinder/paved alley who told me. Another stupid human ending. At least the weeping and wailing, the sniveling and sobbing (as wet as it all was), the words of condolence and sorrow expressed by other family members and visiting neighbors helped strengthened my bricks, my walls, my ceilings, my woodwork.

I'm not quite sure how to label the next group who took over. They were actually part of the G3 group, the grandchildren of the original G3 husband (the one who fell dead in my yard, smashing the tomatoes) and his wife (hit by a truck), but I fear this is getting too complicated, and I am getting tired of making sure you understand. I'll simply let you know when a new group of humans moved in. That new group, the grandchildren, took over as their parents left because they complained there was too much for them to do. For a time, after this change, my upstairs rooms were not rented out. They were needed for the children of the grandchildren (See, even I am confused.). But the garden apartment was always rented out. Various people moved in and out. A father and his unmarried daughter were there for a time. Then another older couple moved in. A young family with three little girls took the apartment, and their constant noise may have annoyed the humans upstairs, but I was happy for the sounds which reinforced and secured the walls and wood in that apartment. They were there a few years, but when they moved, the garden apartment remained empty. Part of the reason was the spurt of neighborhood growth and the availability of additional, new, and updated rental apartments buildings.

The Boulevard told me about the new multi-floor apartment buildings which were sprouting up in the empty lots in the neighborhood. Three of them on the street behind me. Two more on the street behind that one. Across from the median, on the other side of the boulevard, there had been a fire, and the buildings which had burned were torn down and replaced by additional apartment buildings. The neighborhood was changing. More and more cars and trucks and even buses were traveling the boulevard and the main streets. The city was expanding, growing further west, further south, and the result of its growth was that additional humans were crowding in.

Changes were happening close to me too. The yellow brick house to my south had been empty for some time. No humans were there to attend to her, resulting in her appearing abandoned and run-down. Some of her windows had been broken and hastily boarded up. Her front porch steps had chipped concrete. Grass grew tall, and weeds took over. I was relieved when a family obtained her and began to make necessary repairs. Frankly, I was tired of hearing her moaning complaints. We had never been very friendly. After all, I remained rich red brick, and she was now faded, common, yellow brick, although I never held that against her. She could not help the way she had been built. Nevertheless, I was pleased when her windows were replaced and the concrete steps were patched and resurfaced. Her backyard grass was cut and a few small bushes were planted in the front. Her updated looks improved the neighborhood. And as the people in me saw what was happening, the current wife began to complain to the current husband. She wanted to update my insides and change my grassy areas. She wanted to keep up with the neighbors, and I agreed with her.

"Look how perfectly formed those small bushes are," and she leaned over my front porch to view them again, her words floating up to the gutters, containing just a pinch of envy. "We should do something like that, and that tree in the back yard needs trimming too."

The husband continued to read the evening paper and an exasperated sigh left his lips, rushing up to where her words waited, pushing them ever so slightly towards the gutters, acting as if it had been a mistake. The wife glanced at him and then turned to continue her suggestions.

"And the inside of this house hasn't been painted in years. The old refrigerator needs replacing, and those kitchen cabinets need refinishing. I know what that garden apartment looks like, and we can't compete with those new apartments unless we do some upgrades. They are renting for almost twice what we were, and if we raise our rent, that will help pay for all the repairs and replacements. Are you listening to me?"

"Fine," he said. "I'll talk to your uncle who owns that appliance store on twenty-second street and see if he can get us a decent price on the refrigerator."

"Not just that," and the wife's words grew larger and stronger now that she had both his attention and at least a partial concession. "The garden apartment needs upgrades. The stove and refrigerator need replacing. And I absolutely need a new washing machine and want a dryer. We can charge the new tenants to use it, and that will bring in more cash. That would be easier for them than dragging clothes to the laundromat. Don't you think?"

"Sure," and the husband agreed. He wanted to end the discussion, but I knew it was not over. And it wasn't.

It took some weeks, and many more words, but the upgrades started. My walls were repainted, my wooden floors were carefully washed and polished, and new carpeting was put down in both bedrooms. New appliances were installed both in the upstairs kitchen and the downstairs apartment. The cabinets in my kitchen ended up being totally replaced due to the defective refinishing job attempted by the husband who did it himself, trying to save money, and didn't want to tackle the task anyway. A new washer and modern dryer were installed in the basement storage space. The garden apartment was thoroughly cleaned and repainted and its bathroom updated. Landscaping, in the form of small bushes and perennial plants, was completed. The backyard tree was trimmed and looked healthy, and a small garden with a few plants was created beneath the tree. This entire effort took most of the year, and I was pleased when it was finally done. I looked good. Actually, to borrow a word from a long-ago human, I looked *snazzy*.

Once it was all in place, a decision was made. A price for the newly renovated garden apartment was set, and advertising signs were displayed. There was a loud and lengthy discussion about the rental price (Those words fought each other all the way to their places in my ceiling.), and the final decision was to ask for a slightly lesser amount than the newer neighborhood apartments which were filling up fast.

The husband wanted to rent the garden apartment for the same amount as was being asked in the newly built buildings, but the wife thought that a slightly lower monthly rent would attract humans sooner. She was correct. Within a few weeks, the apartment was rented and a young couple moved in. They were Carolyn and Patrick Taylor, and I am giving their names because they are responsible for the fifth hidden secret. Well, Carolyn was. Her husband, Patrick, never knew. I'm not sure he would have cared.

15

Carolyn and Patrick Taylor, 1975

What I have heard:

Carolyn Taylor is twenty-five years old and earns $175.15 a week working at the Fox Family Grocery Store Monday through Friday and sometimes on Saturday. Patrick Taylor is twenty-six years old and earns $223.45 a week at the Wilcoe Manufacturing Company making small machine parts to fit in large machines. They met in high school. Carolyn does the grocery shopping, cooking (including making lunches for both of them), laundry and ironing, cleaning, budgeting and bill paying. Patrick empties the garbage and washes the car. Carolyn is learning to knit and meets with a knitting group every other Tuesday night. On Tuesdays during the fall and winter, Patrick bowls on a team from work, and on Wednesdays during the spring and summer, he plays on a work softball league. At least once each year, he, his father, and brother go on a week-long fishing trip. He brings the caught fish home, and although Carolyn does not eat fish, does not like to see the dead fish, does not appreciate the smell of fish, she cooks it for him. Carolyn just finished reading *Gone with the Wind,* and only needed to renew it once at the local library. Patrick owns over fifty comic books and periodically buys another to add to his collection which he claims will be worth much money someday. Twice a month, on Fridays, the Taylors go to a movie or out to dinner with friends. Some Sundays they go to the late Mass at St. Mary's Catholic Church which is where they were married almost five years ago. During the past four years, Carolyn has been pregnant twice. Last summer, when Patrick was on his fishing trip, she miscarried for the second time, and her mother took her to the hospital and stayed with her until Patrick returned from the fishing trip. She remains heartbroken over the losses. Patrick said it was for the best and not meant to be, and Carolyn was shocked at what she told him was his heartlessness. This led to a loud and spite-filled argument. And after that last fishing trip, she threw the fish away, claiming it had become spoiled.

My observation here: The Taylors were a typical human couple. Except for the last one, the one after the fishing trip, they had few arguments. But the words from that last one grew large and dark and continued fighting as they rose to the garden apartment walls and ceiling. By the time they entered into the cracks and crevices, they were coolly civil, and while they settled close to each other, they never touched. There was a stillness in the apartment for a few days, and then Patrick broke the silence by suggesting they purchase a new and larger television for their entertainment. After it was purchased, the Taylors' conversations, about everything, lessened. At night, when he was home, Patrick watched sports or one of his special programs while Carolyn finished the dishes, made their lunches, and completed necessary laundry or cleaning. On Thursdays Carolyn insisted on watching a family comedy. She liked what she called the *cleverness and humor of the stories*, and although Patrick pretended a disinterest, he watched it with her. On Tuesdays, when she was not with her knitting group, Carolyn watched other shows which Patrick did not like, by herself, while practicing her knitting. Their lives fell into a pattern, and they seemed content. Mostly.

Except for the baby thing. I have observed many humans and formed opinions. While I believe babies unnecessary and can barely tolerate them, I understand the human race depends upon their existence, and adults learn to endure the destruction caused by the young. Structures, such as myself, have no babyhood or youth. When we are built, we are fully grown, and even during the building process, we are sensible enough to avoid self-injury. I cannot say that for the human young who have wandered about my space, running into my walls, falling up and down my stairs, sliding and scratching my floor with their faces and elbows. Bumps and bleeding often appear on their person, but the mutilation to me is unbearable! I have gouges in my woodwork and scarring on my walls. Some windows have been cracked, and while they have been repaired, they still sting. Suffice it to say, children are not my favorite creatures. And yet, knowing all this, realizing all the destruction they cause, Carolyn Taylor desperately wanted one.

"Perhaps a boy and a girl would be nice," she remarked during one night as they were watching a program on the television. "Don't you think so?" She smiled at Patrick and pushed the hair from his face as he turned the pages of a new comic book.

"Um, I guess," and he shifted his head away from her hand.

Carolyn glared at him and sighed. "Sometimes I think you aren't interested in having a family. That just makes me sad," and those words rose with a whiney twist, pulling away from each other, gaining petulancy as they rose.

He let out his own sigh and patted her leg. "Of course I am interested, but really, would it be so bad with just the two of us? Look at Jimmy and Brandi. They are happy without kids and have been married longer than us. I mean, we could travel and get a house, get another car for you, do all sorts of things. Sure, a family would be great, but what if that's not in the cards for us?" These words and sentiments stretched up to the whiney ones, looking parental and slightly threatening, and then reached out to pat them patronizingly on their tops. Reporting this conversation, it occurs to me that similar discussions took place on a monthly basis, for a monthly reason.

Delicate subject. Also, slightly disgusting. Every few weeks, when realizing she would not be a mother, again, Carolyn dissolved into tears. She would be weepy and distressed for a couple days, and then some form of the previously conveyed conversation would occur, often while watching her favorite family comedy. Silence between the Taylors would prevail for a day or two, and their words, when spoken, were formal, edging on stilted anger. Then the feeling of discontent would melt and the remainder of the month would be filled with a sense of hopefulness. At least on Carolyn's part. Another month. More television comedy. Revealing conversations. Frustration and lamentations. I could count on a once-a-month exchange when my walls and ceilings in the garden apartment were filled with the interchange of emotional speech. Annoying, but made me stronger.

And then, one month passed, and Carolyn checked a paper calendar she kept in her top bureau drawer and she smiled. Nothing was said until another month passed, paper calendar noted again, and the bliss on her face almost made me pleased for her. It was at breakfast on a Saturday when she did not have to work that the news was given to Patrick. I will admit, he did an admirable job of seeming happy. He hugged Carolyn, and they discussed the possibility of an increased family over oatmeal and coffee which Carolyn could barely get down. Something was happening to her, and she needed to leave the table twice to rid herself of the few bites she had taken. But, instead of being upset, she returned to the kitchen elated.

"Well, I think that is proof!" and she leaned down to kiss Patrick's cheek as he moved slightly away from the offered kiss. He pushed his half-eaten bowl of cereal to the side, and while his next words appeared to sound delighted, I watched as they floated to the corner of the room, all wearing some sort of mask.

"Well, this will change our lives," and he attempted to make those words appear jovial, but when those masks were removed, they showed their actual feelings: woeful with a touch of grimness. "Will you make a doctor appointment this week? Do you want me to go with you? I'll have to make arrangements with work, and would you not make it Tuesday? I'd like to be at work that day. The guys are planning a poker night, and I'm feeling lucky."

She smiled at him and said, "I'll wait for a week or two to call. The doctor would like me to be closer to three months because of..." and she stopped here, a worried look passing over her otherwise cheerful words. "But that's fine. I am going to go to my knitting group Tuesday. I need to learn how to knit some tiny little booties to cover some tiny little feet. Thinking a soft green or yellow will do for now."

Carolyn stared into space. I assume to picture the tiny yellow or green booties on tiny kicking feet. Again, I almost felt enthused for her. That entire day, she hummed as she cleaned, stopping periodically to look down at her still flat middle, taking an hour to visit a store, returning with a skein of both light yellow and light green yarn. She was joyful and did not notice that the pleased veneer on Patrick's face camouflaged a troubled dread. Dread of fatherhood, perhaps. Depletion of Tuesday and Wednesday night autonomy, maybe. Diminishment of available funds for additional comic book purchases, certainly. But Patrick said all the encouraging words (Fraudulent and fictitious, they hid in the woodwork.) and completed tasks: shoulder rubs, foot massages, ice-cream runs, for the effervescent, exuberant mother-to-be, with just a few words (leaving his mouth and turning disinclined, grudging, unenthusiastic) mumbled to hide his feelings. I waited and watched.

Another month passed. The doctor's appointment was made (not on a Tuesday or Wednesday), and the parents-to-be returned and began to plan the nursery for the second bedroom in my garden apartment. Carolyn gave the exciting news to her family and friends; Patrick mentioned it in passing to his bowling team, and collectively, breaths were held. Carolyn prepared for oncoming motherhood by knitting the light green booties. Unhappy with her first attempt, she pulled out the knitting, rolled up the yarn and started again using the light-yellow yarn. The second attempt was better, and she considered learning to knit a tiny sweater once the booties were completed. But when she finished them, she was not satisfied because the booties appeared uneven, and she pulled out the yarn again. She asked for help from her knitting group, and took her time with this pair, adjusting and counting stitches, measuring the tiny footgear, sighing with anticipation, dreaming of days ahead, and humming tuneless songs. I grew annoyed with her humming as she slowly and cautiously worked the needles, but watched as the wordless sounds gathered strength and rose to spread themselves in the empty spots where actual words were missing.

Her small frame began to fill out, and her growth reminded me of housekeeper #2. Another month passed, and she began a discussion with Patrick about names. He was inattentive because a baseball game was being shown on the television, and that had all his available concentration.

"We could name a girl after my grandmother, *Patricia*, and call her *Patty*. We could even give her your grandmother's name as a middle name, and she would be *Patricia Joanna*. Or maybe *Joan*. *Patricia Joan*. My middle name is *Patricia*, so that would fit. What do you think?"

"Uh Huh," he replied.

"I like the name *Steven* or maybe *Jonathan*, and *Patrick* could be the middle name. I don't think I want *Patrick* as a first name. Wait, were you named after someone in your family?"

There was no answer to this, and Carolyn waited and asked again. Patrick glanced at her and shrugged and gave his full attention to the television. Carolyn started to say something but stopped, sighed, and took up the yellow booties which were almost completed. There were additional attempts to discuss names, to make shopping plans to purchase the best crib, to plan a Christening party in the future. Most of the words spoken during these attempts were Carolyn's, and they all left her mouth exuding cautious excitement and delicate delight, although they were tinged with a hint of apprehension and uncertainty. There had been disaster before. Twice. But when she spoke on the telephone to her friends and her mother, she told them she was feeling fine, and the doctor did not think there were any note-worthy medical issues. She was entering her fifth month and had felt the baby move, so she was thrilled. She was advised to remain careful in her actions, be aware of any unusual changes, and call the doctor in case something unexpected happened.

"I am finishing up the next two weeks at work and then I will be done. Patrick was so excited last night when he held his hand to my middle and could feel the baby moving," and as Carolyn spoke into the telephone, her words wiggled and spun up to the top of the ceiling where they rocked and waddled in a playful manner, eventually settling down, clustering together. "I finished the yellow booties and they look perfect. I am starting a matching sweater, and that's going to be a challenge, but the women at the knitting group said they would help if I got stuck," and she continued to talk about the plans for the second bedroom nursery, the possibility of light-yellow walls, and the continued search for just the right crib and changing table, and all these words filled the air, circling around with restrained elation.

Carolyn spoke with careful constraint to others, but I knew she was worried. On the nights Patrick was playing poker or was with one of his sports leagues, she sat in the front room, television on, although she was inattentive to it. She would hold her hands on her stomach, and whisper to it.

"Oh, little baby," and the murmured words appeared faint and fuzzy, frowning at each other, their demeanors flimsy. "You are so wanted. Please be well. Please!" Tears would roll down her cheeks, and she would wipe them with the backs of her hands. After a time, she would go to the bathroom and splash water on her face. Then she looked into the mirror and polished a smile. Then back to the front room where she picked up the sweater she was knitting and continued working at it. When Patrick came home, she smiled at him, the same smile she practiced in the mirror, and asked how his evening went. I observed her many times. She hid her worries. Not from me. I knew it all.

Carolyn completed her last two weeks at work, and on the last day, she came home with a bag of gifts for the baby. That evening, she held each of them up for Patrick to see, commenting on their use and the delicacy of the bibs, the pacifiers, the small stuffed toys which delighted her as she held them. Patrick didn't seem as delighted, but he nodded and allowed them to fall into his lap as she talked about them.

"Now, we really need to get that nursery done. I am already in the fifth month, and time is going quickly. Oh, look, Patrick, isn't this little stuffed doggie cute? So small! It will just fit into the baby's hands," and Patrick grunted as she first tried to hand the toy to him, and when he didn't take it, she placed it into his lap with the bibs and pacifiers and trinkets for a baby. They stayed there until Carolyn removed them, placing them gently into a large bag. A baseball game was on the television.

Things were fine. Until they weren't. One evening, Patrick came home to find Carolyn sitting at the kitchen table staring into space, the green beans she was trimming, untrimmed.

"Are you ok?" he asked. "Is there something wrong?"

Carolyn looked at him and shook her head. "I just don't feel right," and she placed the paring knife down and sat back. "I don't know what's wrong, but I think something is. My back has hurt all day, and I feel queasy," and those words could barely make it to the kitchen walls. They were puny and strengthless, and a few of them slowly dissipated as I watched.

"Did you call the doctor? Maybe this is just part of being pregnant. Do you want some water or something?"

"No, I didn't call anyone. I wasn't even sure what to say, and I don't have any real symptoms. Just a funny feeling," and she put her hand to her head and rubbed it. "I don't even have dinner ready. Sorry."

Patrick shrugged. "That's fine. Do you want to go out to eat? There is that diner on thirty-fifth street. We could go there. Take a break tonight," and I was surprised at his concern. He was not always so understanding.

"Honestly, I'm not hungry. There are some left-overs, if you are ok with that," and he was. Humans surprise me.

Later that evening, as they were in the front room with the television on, Carolyn spoke again, her words looking scared and solemn.

"There is something else. I have not felt the baby move all day. I was trying to remember the last time I did, and I'm not sure when it was. Maybe yesterday. I don't know. I should have called the doctor, but I didn't. Now I'm worried," and tears pooled in her eyes while her words appeared translucent and watery.

Patrick patted her hand, and spoke, but his eyes never left the television. "Maybe the baby is taking a rest. Wait and see how you feel tomorrow and call the doctor then. I'm sure you are fine."

There was little additional conversation that night, and just a short time later, Carolyn went to bed. She lay in the bed, eyes closed, but not sleeping, and some hours later, Patrick joined her. He fell asleep. She remained awake. The night was quiet; the hours passed. It was just after five o'clock, and the sky outside was just starting to brighten when Carolyn shook Patrick awake.

"Patrick, wake up. Something is wrong. I am bleeding and I feel awful. I think we need to go to the hospital. Please, wake up!"

His eyes slowly opened, and when he saw her standing next to him, he asked, "What time is it? Did you call someone? What do you want again?"

Carolyn was sobbing at this point and that made him sit up. He pulled the covers away and said, "Let me get dressed, and we'll go."

They left in a few minutes, moving rapidly through the apartment and out of the side door. They walked to the car which was parked in front, and Patrick helped Carolyn into the car. He got into the driver's seat, started the car, and pulled quickly away from the curb. It was so early there was little traffic on the streets, and once the car turned the corner, I had no further view of them. The garden apartment was quiet. No noise, no words, no humans. It remained like that for days.

Five days later, the following Monday, the side door opened, and Carolyn and Patrick entered. They were quiet. Patrick placed a white plastic bag down on the floor next to the kitchen table and pulled out a chair for Carolyn who very gingerly sat down. He heated some water and made her a cup of tea, putting it in front of her. Then he sat down across from her. They sat for a time, and Carolyn took a small sip of the tea before looking up at him. Her eyes were dull; her skin appeared sallow, and her middle, while still somewhat puffy, seemed to be droopy. I waited for something to be said, but Patrick got up to pour himself a glass of water, and stood at the sink drinking it. They remained quiet.

I do not pretend to understand the human body and its workings. The subject is not of any interest to me, and other than the importance of human words to my own well-being, to the strengthening of my walls and bricks and wood, to my personal usefulness, I don't care about it. However, observing these two humans, I knew something terrible had occurred. I examined them, their postures, their facial expressions, their silences, and discerned that only two of them had walked through my door and into this space. The soft doggie toy would not be held by small baby hands. There was no baby. And now, I am sure you are feeling sorry for these humans. Don't. You know that your species deals with both appalling and appealing situations often. This one is appalling. I watched the Taylors cope with this: their third loss.

Carolyn remained in bed for a week. Her mother came almost daily. Friends visited and attempted to cheer her up. Patrick brought her flowers one day and a pint of her favorite ice-cream another. She was the center of everyone's attention. But at night, after she went to bed, Patrick remained in the front room with the television on, staring into space, tears forming in his eyes and running down his face. His sobs were not loud, and he always wiped his wet face before joining Carolyn in the bedroom. One night, he found the bag with the bibs, pacifiers, toys for the baby and looked through it. He took it into the second bedroom, the bedroom which had not yet been turned into a nursery, opened the closet door, and shoved it to the back behind some boxes and an old fan. He closed the door. Then he opened it again to look in, and his whispered words ("Can't see it. Good.") rose to the inside of the closet and stuck in the corner. I know what you are thinking, but no, this is not the fifth hidden secret. That will be explained. Actually, when the Taylors moved from my garden apartment, Carolyn found the bag, and once she looked inside, threw the entire thing into the trash.

After some weeks at home, Carolyn left the apartment, and returned with the makings of dinner. When Patrick came home, dinner was ready, and she smiled at him, asking how his day went.

"It was fine. How are you? Feeling better?"

"I am. I went to Foxes today for groceries, and asked for my old job back. I start tomorrow because I need to get back to doing things. I was thinking that we could be careful, save money and in a short time, we might look at getting our own house. There are nice bungalows being built at the southwest end of the city. What do you think?"

Patrick walked over and hugged his wife, and said, "I think that is a great idea. After dinner, let's talk about what we need to do. We already have some money set aside for the…" he stopped, hesitating, scared to complete the thought.

"Yes," Carolyn answered, "I know, and we can add to that now that I will be working again."

The rest of that night, and many nights afterwards, they planned and discussed. Their words filled the walls and ceilings and woodwork with promise and ambition and passion as they rose without hesitation and found places to dwell. Tears were still shed over the loss, but as time went on, both Carolyn and Patrick seemed to heal. Carolyn stopped going to her knitting group and joined a book discussion group at the public library. Patrick, in an attempt to stick to their budget, no longer bought comic books to add to his collection. The Taylors decided that going to dinner or a movie only once a month would be a budget-efficient move. Carolyn began to deep clean the apartment to keep busy, and when she found the half-completed, light-yellow sweater she had been working on, she sat down and stared at it. She began to unravel the sweater, rolling the yarn back up in a ball. She put the yellow yarn along with the green ball of yarn and the knitting needles into a bag and placed it by the side door. She would take the bag to work for Elma, the other cashier. Elma was a knitter. Carolyn knew she would never knit again.

There were a few sleepless nights for Carolyn. On one of those nights, as Patrick was lightly snoring and the kitchen clock showed it was a bit past midnight, she slipped out of bed, thinking she might read for a while. She went to the kitchen for some water, and then to the front room where she picked up her most recent book. As she sat down in the chair, she straightened the cushion and felt something that had fallen in its side. She reached down into the crack and pulled out the yellow booties, the ones she had struggled over, the tiny footwear which was meant to cover the tiny feet of the baby which was no longer a probability. She drew in a deep breath and sat, holding the soft things meant to warm tiny feet, and she cried. The crying was silent, and she used the booties to wipe her tears. She sat staring at them for a long time, and once her tears stopped, she rose from the chair. She took the sweater which was hanging on a chair and slipped it on. Walking over to the back door leading out to the back yard, she found the shoes she left there and pushed her feet into them. There was a flashlight next to the washing machine. She took it, turned it on, and quietly opened the door to the yard. It was dark and still, and she used the flashlight to find the garden tool left next to the bricks in the back. She picked up the trowel and moved to the one tree in my backyard. The tree which has a small garden underneath it. She positioned the flashlight so that she could see what she needed to. She began.

In the darkness, with just the small beam of light placed next to the garden under the tree, Carolyn began to dig. She moved some of the perennials over and using the trowel, dug a deep small hole. A hole deep enough to place a pair of tiny light-yellow booties meant for a baby who would never be. When the hole was deep enough, she took the booties she had knitted, the ones she had sighed and labored over and kissed them. Then she pressed them down into the hole she had dug with the garden trowel. Forcing them down, she dug an even deeper hole with her fingers, not caring that the dirt was beneath her fingernails. She took the flashlight and looked down at the booties. Just a speck of the yellow could be seen shining up through the dirt, the soil, the grime. And then, ignoring the trowel, using her hands, she moved the loose soil over the hole, packing it around the minuscule yellow, pushing it down so that nothing could be seen of the knitted item. Mushing the dirt flat, readjusting the plants over the hole, she stood and flashed the beam of light over the grave she had dug. She was satisfied. It would not be noticed. She stood for a time, breathing in the night air before returning the trowel to its place, re-entering the basement, washing her hands, brushing dirt from her nightclothes and, after completing these tasks, she lowered herself carefully into the bed. Nothing was ever said to Patrick. And in less than a year, the Taylors had saved the money for the down payment of their new bungalow, and moved out of my basement garden apartment taking the furniture, the television, and Patrick's comic book collection with them.

So, there it is, the fifth secret. The secret no one will ever uncover. No one will ever find. What happens to soft yellow yarn when it is buried in a hole, covered with dirt, left for decades? Does it disintegrate? Will it decay? Is it possible for the whole to become dismantled, to disperse into tinier yellow pieces of fluff? If someone were to dig up that garden, to turn the soil over, to actually find the mystery, would there be minuscule brightness to catch their eye? Would the booties stay intact, and if cleaned, if carefully washed and lovingly dried, would the small items still fit on the tiny feet of a baby who was present? I suppose it does not matter. No one has ever found the knitted footwear. No one ever will. Even if you, the reader, came to my backyard, that garden under the tree is gone. You would be stymied by not knowing where to place your shovel. You would need to dig up patch after patch, removing weeds and grass trying to discover the hole. It would be useless. Don't bother. This is one secret which will remain concealed. But now, reader, you know what it is.

16

The Last...
really there is one more...Secret

Well, there it is. My history to date, and the secrets I promised to tell. Surprise! There is one more, and I will get to that. Be warned that this secret is not a tangible, physical artifact as were the others. This secret is not hidden in me. It IS me. Interested? Intrigued?

I am entering my third century. Families have moved in and out, and I have undergone many changes. My walls were often repainted; the garden in the back was torn up and replaced with grass; the garage housed various makes and models of cars. Time passed. The neighborhood endured additional changes: new buildings, added businesses, more and more humans. Eventually, a *For Sale* sign was placed in my front yard, but no one came, and I remained empty for perhaps a dozen years or so. People would appear to look around my insides, walk through the garden apartment, open and close my closet doors, but no one moved in. I was alone. Not that I minded. I have all the words and emotions, all the deeds and actions I need to hold my walls, my bricks in place for decades. Sometimes I pull out some words and emotions and listen to them, remember their origins, all of them just as vibrant as when first created. I play with them. I set one group against another just to see their reactions. The word groups were usually puzzled, especially if they were decades apart. Word meanings change over time, and the word groups were mostly confused. Emotions? They may have been decades apart, but anger is anger and joy is joy. Those did not change. There was humor in watching it, in amusing myself. If I could have laughed, I would have.

Recent changes have occurred. There is movement, and the feeling of excitement throughout my space. A new couple is here. A young couple who could afford to attain me and intend to renovate me. They will bring me into the twenty-first century, so they claim. After being so empty, I look forward to watching their words fill up the areas which remain blank. Their emotions will seep into the gaps and crowd into vacant territory. Don't worry, there is plenty of space left. The words which are there will just move back for them; they will make way; they might even welcome the newness.

The new humans did not immediately move in, but began their work by updating my exterior. Tuck pointing was completed. I have a new roof, and most of my windows have been replaced. New doors, back and front, were constructed, and special locks are in place. The walkway to the back, the one which leads to the garage, was cracked and in pieces. It is newly repaired, and the garage has also been reinforced and strengthened. I must admit, it looks snazzy, like a bowtie someone once bought and wore. The concrete on my front steps has been power-washed and resurfaced and sealed. Looks better than new. The garden apartment door was replaced, and the patio in the back was mended. Even the tree in the back yard was pruned, and grass seed was placed where needed. It all feels good.

Now they are working on finishing my interior. I listen as they plan what to do, and their words are so filled with excitement and eagerness that they fly up to the ceiling, burrow into the plaster, find a tidy space, and wait for additional words. Hope does that. The humans started in the second bedroom. Walls were in good shape, and they simply cleaned and painted and put in some new carpeting. Then they worked at the downstairs bathroom. The woman was delighted with the claw-footed bathtub saying, "I LOVE this. It's perfect, and I can't wait to take a bath in it. So authentic!" She is correct. You should have seen *those* words fly up! The bathroom took a while because there were some plumbing issues which needed attention, and I am glad they did not hurry but did it correctly. These humans may not be as bad as some who were here in the past. Currently, they are working in my kitchen. The old linoleum is pulled up, replaced by some new type of flooring. I am unfamiliar with this and will need to inspect it carefully, but the humans seem pleased by the looks. They believe they will complete the kitchen in about three weeks. Recently, they decided to move in and live in me while continuing the work. They set up their space in the second bedroom, and work at fixing the rest of me after they return from their jobs. They are active during nights and weekends. A year, they think, and I will be finished. There are plans to eventually make the upstairs rooms part of the family space. They discuss how the garden apartment will be revised and that they plan to rent it out, but that is sometime in the future. Talks about having a family are periodically heard. I suppose that means children, and while I am not looking forward to that, I have been subjected to them before, and will adjust. Numerous times, they have remarked that I am *structurally sound*. Ha! Of course I am.

I wonder if in all this revising and renovating they will discover the hidden secrets. Three of them are upstairs and they have not begun to work up there. One is in the basement, and that remodeling will also take place in the future. I doubt the yellow baby booties, which have been in the dirt for so many years, are even discoverable, but who knows? What would they think about these curiosities? They will never know the entire stories although those words and emotions and sounds are sequestered in me. In my bricks and walls and woodwork and flooring and plaster. Safe in me. Known to nobody. Except me. And, of course, now, you.

I listen to these humans at night while they are in the bedroom discussing me. They are constantly asking each other, *What do you think of…* and *Should we do this…* and *What is the cost if we…* Then they grow silent; he looks at some papers; she reads a book or glances through some house decorating magazine, and in that silence, I can hear some of the words in the wall and bricks becoming restless. They may utter, exclaim, express because they are so used to me allowing that to occur. And there are times they are heard by the humans as they lay in their bed reading, allowing the narrowly muted words to surround them. It startles them.

"Did you hear that?" she asks.

"What?"

"Listen, there are sounds or maybe words I can hear. Listen."

The humans are hushed and still and attentive while the words jostle the emotions close to them making sounds suggesting a conversation. The woman is much more sensitive to these things. The man pretends to hear nothing although I can see his eye twitch and sometimes, he sticks a finger in his ear and shakes it as though the issue is inside his head.

"This is an old house," he comments, "It's settling noises. That's all. Don't worry about it. What do you think…that there are *ghosts?*" and he gives a laugh which comes shakily from his mouth and wobbles all the way to the ceiling.

"Well, no," she answers, "At least I hope not." She moves closer to him and his arm slinks around her and they continue the reading. But she keeps her ears attuned to the sounds. She does not believe in ghosts, but this house is so old, and…

As they work in me, cleaning and repairing and changing, they talk and wonder about me. About those who lived here before them. About the things which may have happened over the last century. About the possibilities of love and hate, of anger and joy. The wife stopped once, turned and looked around and remarked to the husband, "If these walls could speak, think of the tales they could tell," and I wanted to laugh and hoot at that comment.

And now, here it is: the last secret. Just for you. Have you ever heard those strange sounds in your own place of residence in the night when you are in bed, just before you are ready to fall asleep? Do your eyes pop open and then close tightly while you pull the cover over your head? Do you do this and feel silly? Apprehensive? Jittery? Do you, especially if you are alone, think you should get out of bed and check, and if you are brave enough to do so and find nothing there, quickly jump back into the bed, still warm from your body and immediately shut your eyes? You aren't alone. The sounds are also heard in all public buildings, like banks and stores and schools, but ignored because daily human noises muffle them. But when those buildings are emptied at night except for a night watchman or guard, the words are heeded. Humans who may be there are startled, panicked, disconcerted. They tell themselves: *Don't be a baby. Go and check it out. It is nothing. This building is old. It is settling, that's all. There are no ghosts.* And there are not. The sounds heard are not ghosts. That is a made-up human concept, a false abstraction. There are no ghosts. Never have been. Never will be.

Those disquieting, unsettling, unnerving sounds are the words the emotions, the stories which are trapped in your house or apartment or condominium, or rented room, or hotel room. Words and emotions and deeds and lives are in each and every building and living space. All of them. They are in the brick-and-mortar houses, in those which have siding, in wooden cabins, in caves and caravans, in round homes and underground homes, in igloos and house boats, in Honai homes and tree houses, in Pueblo homes and turf houses, in tents and chalets, stone cottages, thatched homes, castles and riads. Words and emotions and deeds hold the living spaces upright, and even if the buildings are new, some humans built them: placed the bricks, formed the mud balls, cut the ice blocks. The builders' words, feelings, sounds do not leave. They remain. They are everlasting and enduring and endless. If you listen carefully, if you are attentive to the peeps, the creaks, the clashes, the crunches, if you do not ignore the vibrations which are there for you to discover and attend to, you will know what they are, will realize their importance, will appreciate their history. You may even realize the tales. Will they frighten you? Possibly. After all, you are only human.

This is all I have to tell you. This is truly the last secret. Perhaps there will be additional stories in another hundred years; perhaps not.

Humans are just not that interesting, not that important, not that special. Not like a red-brick building. But there you are. You now know about the room, the apartment, the house, where you are, where you live, and sleep, and speak, and worry, and love, and hate. You know that your words and emotions and deeds are never lost, never disappear, never forgotten, even when you are. And you will be. Oh yes, you, all humans, will be.

I am like the house to my north and the one to my south. I am connected to the alley and the street and the parkway and the boulevard. We all know this secret. We are all the same. We are bystanders. We are spectators. We are beholders.

We are not judges. We are not juries. We are observers. We are onlookers. We are witnesses. We are viewers, watchers.

We are recipients of the deeds.
We are inheritors of all words.
We are keepers of secrets.
We are.

I AM.

Acknowledgments

First: to some of the humans who helped me through the decades…not all of you…many of you were sloppy and careless, but to the few who were not, I am pleased with your behavior. Of course, you owe me more. I kept you dry in the rain and warm in the snow and cool in the summer. I protected you.

Then to the City of Chicago: Finally! You are starting to care for and clean up the boulevard, the crosswalk, the street, the parkway. It's about time. Please hurry. You have been lazy.

Lastly to my co-author: Susan M. Szurek. (Why she insists upon that silly middle initial, I will never know. Humans!) Anyway, I'd like to say…um…the word is difficult, but I will reach into a brick…just…there…and pull out a word from Babcia: Dziekuje.

(By the way, any and all mistakes are my co-author's.)

Red-Brick House